A 21 DAY JOURNEY OF RESTORATION & TRANSFORMATION

A Daniel Fast For Rain

FATHER, SEND YOUR RAIN!

LORD JESUS, SEND YOUR RAIN!

HOLY SPIRIT, WE NEED YOUR RAIN!

DEDICATION

This "journey" is dedicated to The Greatest Promise Christ gave to us: The Holy Spirit. To Joyce Mitchell who was used by the Holy Spirit to challenge and encourage me to provide direction and structure for a 21 Day Daniel Fast. *To the faithful followers of Christ of Freely Forgiven Community Church who give me the precious privilege to be a facilitator and S.E.E.R. of PAPA God's Designed Destiny and Vision for their lives.* Finally, to all those individuals, churches and families that took the "first" 21 Day Journey – may the rain of restoration and transformation keep falling on your "fields."

A 21 DAY JOURNEY OF RESTORATION & TRANSFORMATION

A Daniel Fast For Rain

by

R. EARL BROWN

Giving People Hope International Ministries

P.O. Box 92893

Lakeland, Florida 33804-2893

863-808-9596

www.hopecoaching.org

Copyright © 2008 by R. Earl Brown

A WORD OF THANKS

First and foremost, I give thanks to the Holy Spirit, my Senior Partner. There are so many people to give thanks to PAPA God for, for the completion of this Manual. However, I especially want to give thanks for my wife Linda for staying faithful to *"God's foolishness"* as I yearn to hear, receive, and obey instructions from His mouth. I give thanks for Mrs. LaVonne Barnaby for tirelessly typing the first version of the manual and all the extra work she did, without being asked. I give thanks to Pastor Letitia Stones for creating the cover design and Traci Carroll for designing the rest of this manual. I give thanks for all the Pastors who heard the voice of the Holy Spirit and joined in the first 21 Day Journey using the original 40 page manual. I give very special thanks for Pastor Pearce Ewing and his wife Dorothy of New Bethel AME, Lakeland, Florida and Father Wade Fahnestock of First Christian Church, Lakeland, Florida who opened their doors for the 6:00PM-9:00PM prayer, thanksgiving, praise and worship. Thank you to Pastor Selwyn and Prophetess Greta Moran who not only heard the voice of the Holy Spirit, they encouraged three or more churches to become involved in the first 21 Day Journey. To my covenant friend and intercessor, Pastor Jonathan Govender of Pietermaritzburg, South Africa for praying for me and being obedient to phone and confirm God's desire for this journey. I want to give exceeding thanks for my new spiritual Dad and Mom in Polk County, Bishop Jerry and Pastor Shelby Hayes of New Testament Church of God, Auburndale, Florida. Finally, I give thanks to all the individuals and families around the country, you know who you are, who participated in the first 21 Day Journey. Your encouragement and feedback inspired us to move forward expeditiously in bringing this revised manual to a wider audience.

WHAT OTHERS HAVE EXPERIENCED ON THE JOURNEY

The impact of this 21 Day Daniel fast of restoration and transformation has been the movement of the Holy Spirit. He is stirring the hearts of people to move out of their comfort zone and into God's comfort zone, and be willing to win the lost at any cost. He is saying, *"I beseech you therefore brethren, by the mercies of God, that ye present your bodies a living sacrifice, holy, acceptable unto God, which is your reasonable service. And be not conformed to this world: but be ye transformed by the renewing of your mind, that ye may prove what is that good, and acceptable, and perfect, will of God"* (Romans 12:1, 2). Each day we pray for the rain of the Holy Spirit upon our families, churches and communities. We pray for the rain of the Spirit of Truth. We pray for Pastors after God's heart, to do His will, and Christians called to action and for Christians and sinners to come to repentance. We thank Dr. R. Earl Brown for his obedience and dedication to Father God and for bringing us on this journey with him: *"For it is God which worketh in you, both to will and to do His good pleasure"* (Philippians 2:13).

– Bishop Jerry W. Hayes, Pastor
The Church of God of Auburndale, Inc.
Auburndale, Florida

God has called us to separate from the world and draw nigh to Him. This Daniel Fast is not just to change our diet (food), but to change our lifestyle and our way of thinking. Daniel was placed with the Prince of Eunuchs. In ancient times eunuchs were placed in important positions in the Kings House (palace).... Daniel was no doubt a busy man; yet, he found time to seek the Lord.... Jesus said in Matthew 19:12 that some made themselves eunuchs for the Kingdom of God. One lesson we are learning, we do not have to become eunuchs, but we must separate ourselves unto the Lord to do the "King's Business." Dr. Brown, thank you for your labor and for sharing with us this 21 day journey.

– Bishop Milton G. Miller, Assistant Pastor
The Church of God of Auburndale, Inc.
Auburndale, Florida

> *One lesson we are learning, we do not have to become eunuchs, but we must separate ourselves unto the Lord to do the "King's Business."*

Since I started the 21 day journey, God has truly blessed me and my family. When I read the word it comes alive before my eyes. When I'm reading the Word, I have a better understanding of what the writer is saying to me. I praise God for Jesus! Some time I get up and run from the excitement. What captured my attention in the Book of John was when Lazarus died and Jesus heard about it. The Bible said that He moaned in His spirit and even wept. What compassion He has for His people. After He told Lazarus to "come forth" He told them to "loose him" of the bondage of his grave clothes. It makes me think that He not only wants to save us but to free us of our bondages. What manner of man is this that He would give His life for someone like me! Glory to God! Several of the guys at work ask me questions concerning problems in their lives and the Holy Spirit has used me as a vessel to help them with answers that only God Himself could have provided. LET IT RAIN, LET IT RAIN, LET IT RAIN!!!

– R. Dixon
Atlanta, Georgia

… I have been journaling thus far as God has truly been speaking to me…. At the 7 day mark, He has impressed upon me that I am going through a process of spiritual emptying…. While our physical bodies are going through a process of cleansing and emptying the various toxins and waste out of our system, our spiritual man is going through the same process. My God, the spiritual toxins that are being emptied out of me are horrendous! I am so humbled as I cannot imagine any of my brothers and sisters doing "ministry" with the things we harbor within us that we are unaware of that makes us far less effective in doing "His" work because we are unaware of spiritual contaminants. Do I like what he has revealed to me? Not at all! However, because He has revealed this to me, I now have a choice to conform my mind, my character and my will unto His "divine" plan for my life and the lives of others…. As I go through this process, I am reminded of the importance that my belief system be totally in alignment with His. It is becoming more emphatically important to me that I not believe just because of the signs and wonders but because He is the Christ…. My God, when I think of His favor upon my life, it calls me to worship Him because it's of no righteousness of my own, but it is truly His. That's what has increased my worship….

– Cheryl Hurley
Daughters of Deliverance
Philadelphia, Pennsylvania

I have learned not to delay obedience to God, but to swiftly move when He gives a command. Also, I prayed for the Holy Spirit to give me my orders for my divine purpose…

This part of my testimony I was going to keep back because I was embarrassed but the Holy Spirit led me to share. *"There is therefore now no condemnation to them which are in Christ Jesus, who walk not after the flesh, but after the Spirit"* (Romans 8:1 KJV). I was in a relationship with a young man that wasn't of God. He is separated from his wife but not divorced. We had been involved intimately for awhile. God had told me to end the physical part of the relationship months before the fast and I did. Then He told me to end the relationship itself. I was disobedient and didn't let go. The second or third day of the fast God told me to tell him we needed to part company, and I did. I felt such a weight lift off of me. I have learned not to delay obedience to God, but to swiftly move when He gives a command. Also, I prayed for the Holy Spirit to give me my orders for my divine purpose – this was day 9 of the fast. It seemed as if He spoke to me within minutes of my request. He told me what my assignment is to be!!!

– R. Cooper
Lakeland, Florida

The 21 Day Daniel fast and especially the seven days at our church touched me with the love of God, understanding and wisdom. Even though I am a Caucasian, I had child-like dreams and visions within me of a musical heritage rooted deep in the African heritage of the Church. Those seven days of the 21 Day Journey of Restoration and Transformation allowed me to know deep within that we are one, brothers and sisters, in one God, one Son, and one Holy Spirit. God has given us freedom and peace and this journey of restoration and transformation should not end. The City of Lakeland can live out the dream of Martin Luther King, Jr.

– René Godbout
Lakeland, Florida

Thank You PAPA God for Pastor Earl, my husband, Pastor, closest friend and master motivator, who heard and heeded the instructions from Your mouth regarding this 21 Day Journey of Restoration and Transformation. As one song writer said, "I will never be the same again…." My blessings started before the journey, during the preparation time, listening and watching people in our church get excited and ready. For many, it was their very first time on a Daniel fast. They asked so many questions and some took the manual to the grocery store to shop. I was truly blessed by their passion and willingness. Then, there was the music. For the first time in my life singing, worshiping, praising, playing for three weeks straight, and the Lord God Almighty rained on me – blessed me with four new songs. My voice was sustained and I attended every night with such an expectation. I continue to believe to see all that God is going to do to His glory. So Lord, LET IT RAIN!

– Linda K. Brown, Worship Pastor
Freely Forgiven Community Church
Lakeland, Florida

Earl… I want to thank you for your obedience to the Holy Spirit in calling the Daniel fast and season of prayer. I know it was purposeful in His unfolding plan to bring revival to our city – and it was also divinely purposeful in His purposes for me and my family. Your e-mail to me in August inspired me to come to the KBN lunch on August 26th and hear about fasting and prayer. Naomi had just been discharged from the hospital the day before… so I was just beginning a downward spiral myself when I came to the KBN lunch. When you explained that fasting "puts us in a position to hear from God," I knew right away that I needed to fast – and to hear from Him. When Naomi came home from the hospital (the day before the KBN luncheon) I found out that they had put her on Zoloft and an intense rage came over me and I was very unkind (to say the least) toward Naomi about the matter. I found myself very threatened by her condition and the need for that kind of medication. It seemed to me that every time we (or I) tried to move ahead in ministry, Naomi would end up in a similar situation (i.e., an anxiety episode) and everything would come to a halt (this also happened in 2005 and back in 1998). Anyway, I found myself taking out my fears and frustrations on Naomi and was beside myself with anger at her – and at the same time, a tremendous amount of guilt for treating her so badly. I argued with her at length that she didn't need Zoloft and put a tremendous amount of pressure on her. I just couldn't accept the fact that she 'came apart' again. Through all of this, The Lord was dealing with my fears and self-centeredness. Anyway, the call to fast and pray was timely and essential, both for the fulfillment of God's word for the city and for me personally. Naomi got worse over the next two weeks and you saw her condition first hand when we came for prayer. I knew by that point that our only hope was prayer and fasting (Matt. 17:21). When she received prayer that Sunday night at your office, faith welled up in me that the Lord was doing something significant – and He did. The tormenter was cast out…. Her mind and spirit have been strong since the deliverance and the Lord is doing a wonderful work in us and in our marriage. I could probably write more about this but I will just end here to say that we thank and appreciate you and Linda for being obedient and available for us. God has used you to bless us greatly.

– Paul, your fellow servant and laborer in the Lord
Lakeland, Florida

> …the call to fast and pray was timely and essential, both for the fulfillment of God's word for the city and for me personally.

OUR CRY:

Heavenly Father, send an outpouring of Holy Spirit
rain and the rain of your Word that unleashes a God
invasion of family and community restoration and
transformation.

TABLE OF CONTENTS

FOREWORD

Intimate friendship with God! Oh what an outstanding concept. The more we understand what God is really like; the prospect of the fulfillment of the concept becomes most exciting. To have an exuding acquaintance with the creator of the universe is no small thought. However, to be on intimate terms with him is a blessing of monumental magnitude and enough contemplation to keep our hearts fluttering for the rest of our lives.

Multitudes of people around the globe believe God is the creator of the universe, but very few enjoy the wonderful relationship with Him as Father which is where intimacy starts. I have read of many individuals that have been anointed and exceptionally powerful. All of them have been very intimate with God. For example, consider the life of Elijah and think of the great exploits of his life. One scholar said that there was nothing special about Elijah- his background, culture, history or city. Elijah was a Tishbite of the inhabitants of Gilead. The Tishbites were one of the most insignificant of the Israelites. Gilead was the backside of nowhere. Yet, he walked to the front stage of history and single-handedly brought down the terrorist network of Ahab and Jezebel. He shut up Heaven, put the keys in his pocket and walked away without even asking God's permission. Elijah was able to do all that he did, because He was intimate enough to know and be acquainted with the will of God. James tells us that he was a man very much like all ordinary men. However, his prayer and his intimacy with God set him apart from ordinary men.

The excitement and fulfillment that comes from experiencing close friendship with God has to start with becoming part of God's family and God has no grandchildren. Therefore, we have to be individually linked to him through a personal relationship through His son, the Lord Jesus Christ. The first book of Daniel explains a peculiar phenomenon. Daniel and his colleagues refuse to eat the king's meat or to partake of his wine which they were to enjoy for three years. Instead, they gave themselves to prayer and fasting. At the end of only ten days they were looking more well-nourished and much wiser than all those who participated in the king's wine and meat. The king's meat speaks of his doctrine and the king's wine is the spirit of Babylon.

> *Many modern Christians are practicing the Daniel fast for their breakthrough.*

Many modern Christians around the globe are practicing and participating in the Daniel fast for their breakthrough. I have been practicing the Daniel fast for approximately two years, but I had no specific guidelines. Recently, I visited Dr. and Mrs. Earl Brown's home in Davenport, Florida. Not only were they on the Daniel fast, Dr. Brown had created a manual that provided many Biblio-centric principles for this fast. I was completely blown away when I read it. I expressed my profound appreciation for the manual and Dr. Brown asked me to do this foreword to the revision, to which I respond with alacrity. I would like to encourage everyone who picks up a copy of this book: *Your life is about to be changed for good – forever.* Dr. Brown has taken time and diligence to design the blue print with simplicity for anyone beginning a life of prayer and fasting or for the seasoned saint. I truly believe this is part of his assignment in the body of Christ.

– Bishop J. Francis
Monument Of Faith
Miami, Florida

PREFACE

This manual was originally written to provide direction and guidance for a 21 day Daniel fast from August 31 - September 20, 2008, primarily for churches in Lakeland and Polk County, Florida. However, when people heard about or read the manual, churches and families as far away as South Africa became interested. When I finished the first manual I knew I was to expand it for future use; but, my thoughts were on our church and the prophetic word spoken over Lakeland and the City's role in the global end-time harvest. Only God could have created such a desire for a manual that had so many errors and flaws. People's hearts are being enlarged by God to desire real restoration and transformation. Hence, they looked beyond the Manual's faults and saw their need and the timing of God to *"...Ask the Lord for rain..."* (Zech. 10:1a).

As the reports and testimonies started pouring in many confirmed my sense that the manual could be revised to become a "journey" that individuals, families, congregations, groups within congregations (e.g. youth, men, women, key leaders, etc.), and even businesses would be able to use to challenge their employees to experience dynamic restoration and transformation – *personally and professionally*. This is the *season of the saints* and the call to ascend the heights of our assigned mountain demand far more than we can acquire from the natural realm. The primary purpose of fasting is to draw us from the natural into the spiritual. Like Daniel and his three friends, fasting is designed to stimulate the spiritual faculties of *"those who have purposed"* to go on a journey in the passionate pursuit of pleasing God. Fasting is the *"master key to the impossible,"* because it empowers you to strengthen and implement prayer and your relationship with the Holy Spirit. The Holy Spirit is the One Who provided all the knowledge, skill in learning, wisdom, and understanding to Daniel and his friends. The Holy Spirit lives and walks in you: *fasting helps to increase your intimacy with Him.*

> *...fasting helps to increase your intimacy with Him.*

In *Shaping History Through Fasting and Prayer,* Derek Prince *"hits the nail on the head"* when he states *"... Fasting deals with the two great barriers to the Holy Spirit that is erected by man's carnal nature. These are the stubborn self-will of the soul and the insistent self gratifying appetites of the body. Rightly practiced, fasting brings both soul and body into subjection to the Holy Spirit"* (p. 86). For this reason the enemy of your soul will fight you from pursuing this *"21 Day Journey of Restoration and Transformation."* Dare to pursue this journey with your whole heart and with intensity and sincerity and PAPA God has promised you that He will: *"In just a short time restore you, so that you may live in His presence"* (paraphrase of Hosea 6:2). Therefore your heart's cry throughout this journey must be *"Oh, that we might know the Lord! Let us press on to know him. He will respond to us as surely as the arrival of dawn or the coming of rains in the early spring"* (Hosea 6:3).

Rain represents the sufficient blessings and power to empower one to mature in Christ and fulfill one's Designed Destiny. Some definitions of rain according to The New Strong's Exhaustive Concordance of the Bible include: To cause to rain, the spring rain; the latter rain; (eloquence); to gather the after crop; latter growth; to flow as water; to point (as if aiming the finger); to teach; teacher; to direct; to inform; to instruct; a sprinkling (the former or first rain); to shower violently; an archer.

The time for tips and techniques is over! People need to be taught and *know how to walk with God!* In order to gather in the after crop, this great latter growth of nations coming to Christ will demand nothing less than an outpouring of the rain of the Holy Spirit and the rain of His word so that restored and transformed people teach, direct, inform, and instruct by precept and example under the guidance and leadership of the Holy Spirit. There is a far better principle than the familiar "Give people a fish and you feed them for a day; teach people to fish and you feed them for a lifetime." In this prophetic timing of God, we must be vigilant to understand that when we teach people a rule we help them solve a problem; *teach people to walk with God and we help them solve the rest of their life.*

This season of seeking God through the *21 Day Journey of Restoration and Transformation* is about understanding and practically walking out a process to ensure and enhance the level of intimacy with God that empowers you to live **NOT YOUR BEST LIFE**; but, **the life God designed**

> **This season of seeking God empowers you to live the life God designed for you.**

and made ready for you to live (see Ps. 139:13-16; Eccl. 3:11; Eph 2:10; 1 Cor. 2:9-16). To this end, I strongly encourage you to acquire a teaching to study before or after you complete this journey entitled *"The Call of the Kingdom: Intimacy – Inner Strength – Impact"* by Pastor Leticia Stones. This journey will help you to increase your intimacy with God, your inner strength, and your ability to have Kingdom impact. I guarantee you that Pastor Letitia's teaching will get you and keep you supercharged to desire even more intimacy, inner strength, and impact.

It is my sincere desire and prayer that every person, every family, every church, group of churches, businesses, and whosoever will embark upon this journey will receive as their reward *NOT* what I promise; but, what PAPA God has declared and decreed for those who follow His principle and pattern for repentance that leads to restoration, transformation and revival. Remember: *"And it is impossible to please God without faith. Anyone who wants to come to him must believe that God exists and that he rewards those who sincerely seek him"* (Heb. 11:6). In order to experience the rain of restoration and transformation in your life, your family, your church, your business, or whatever group you have chosen to take this journey with, you must have faith in the God of Daniel and the fact that this is and was *NOT a diet or a lifestyle.* This purpose-driven fast was Daniel's chosen pattern to meet PAPA God's requirement found in 2 Chronicles 7:14: *"Then if my people who are called by my name will humble themselves and pray and seek my face and turn from their wicked ways, I will hear from heaven and will forgive their sins and restore their land."* PAPA God has promised that when His people will *humble themselves, pray, seek His face,* and *turn from their wicked ways;* He will *hear, forgive,* and *restore.* **To "seek His face" is to "have a conversation."** The single most powerful vehicle to meet *our four requirements* is *united fasting and prayer.* The purpose driven fast of Daniel fits the bill when combined with increased prayer, thanksgiving, praise, and worship. Daniel 10:2-3 shows us that His purpose driven fast of chapter one was a pattern for him when he desired to humble himself, pray, seek God's face, and turn from his wicked ways: **"When this vision came to me, I, Daniel, had been mourning for three whole weeks.** *All that time I had eaten no rich food. No meat or wine crossed my lips* and I used no fragrant lotions until those three weeks had passed"** (emphasis added).

We are commanded by Christ to personal and united fasting and prayer. Therefore, if Daniel was called by God *"greatly beloved"* or *"very precious to God"* and his purpose driven fast obtained such powerful results, how much more will PAPA God hear, forgive, and restore when we with intensity and sincerity commit to this *"21 Day Journey of Restoration and Transformation."* Hear what PAPA God says about you:

> ***...to the praise of the glory of His grace, by which He made us accepted in the Beloved.*** Ephesians 1:6 (NKJV)

> ***Therefore, as the elect of God, holy and beloved, ...*** Colossians 3:12 (NKJV)

The most important factor is the motive for which you set out on this journey. Christ made this very clear in Matthew 6:1-18 when He gave His instructions to His disciples concerning three related requirements: *giving alms, praying, and fasting.* For the purpose of this journey I desire to make you aware of Christ command for personal prayer, united prayer, as well as united prayer and fasting. He gave direction for personal prayer: ***"When thou [singular] prayest...."*** He also gave direction for united prayer: ***"When ye [plural] pray...."*** Furthermore, He gave directions for both personal and united fasting. ***"When thou [singular] fastest..."*** speaks to the individual. ***"When ye [plural] fast..."*** speaks to a group meeting together for a united fast.

> *The most important factor is the motive for which you set out on this journey.*

Finally, the reason why this *21 Day Journey of Restoration and Transformation* is a seed to impact families and communities is because it is a pattern that has been proven in the Word of God to fully apply the prayer principle found in Matthew 18: 18-20 (AMP):

> **18)** *Truly I tell you, whatever you forbid and declare to be improper and unlawful on earth must be what is already forbidden in heaven, and whatever you permit and declare proper and lawful on earth must be what is already permitted in heaven.*

> **19)** *Again I tell you, if two of you on earth agree (harmonize together, make a symphony together) about whatever [anything and everything] they may ask, it will come to pass and be done for them by My Father in heaven.*

> **20)** *For wherever two or three are gathered (drawn together as My followers) in (into) My name, there I AM in the midst of them.*

I heard someone say "You become intimate [harmonize and make a symphony] with the One you pray to, the one you pray for and the one you pray with. Dare to take this journey – *someone, somewhere is waiting for your restoration and transformation.* Remember, the 21 day journey is not an end – it is the beginning of your increased intimacy with PAPA God, inner strength, and restoration and transformation to have Kingdom impact. For *"...the people who know their God, shall prove themselves strong and shall stand firm and do exploits [for God]* (Daniel 11:32b).

FOUNDATIONAL PROMISES WE PURSUE

"Sow for yourselves according to righteousness, uprightness and right standing with God; reap according to mercy and loving kindness. Break up your uncultivated ground, for it is time to seek the Lord, to inquire of Him and to require His favor, till He comes and teaches you righteousness and rains His righteous gift of salvation upon you." **Hosea 10:12 (AMP)**

"Be glad then, you children of Zion, and rejoice in the Lord, your God; for He gives you the former or early rain in just measure and in righteousness, and He causes to come down for you the rain, the former rain and the latter rain, as before .... And I will restore or replace for you the years that the locust has eaten. The hopping locust, the stripping locust, and the crawling locust, My great army which I sent among you." **Joel 2:11-30 (Hear 23, 25) (AMP)**

"ASK OF the Lord rain in the time of the latter or spring rain. It is the Lord Who makes lightnings which usher in the rain and give men showers, and grass to everyone in the field." **Zechariah 10:1**

PRAYER OF RESTORATION

PSALMS 80 AMP

1) *GIVE EAR, O Shepherd of Israel, You Who lead Joseph like a flock; You Who sit enthroned upon the cherubim [of the ark of the covenant]; shine forth*

2) *Before Ephraim and Benjamin and Manasseh! Stir up Your might, and come to save us!*

3) *Restore us again, O God; and cause Your face to shine [in pleasure and approval on us], and we shall be saved!*

4) *O Lord God of hosts, how long will You be angry with Your people's prayers?*

5) *You have fed them with the bread of tears, and You have given them tears to drink in large measure.*

6) *You make us a strife and scorn to our neighbors, and our enemies laugh among themselves.*

7) *Restore us again, O God of hosts; and cause Your face to shine [upon us with favor as of old], and we shall be saved!*

8) *You brought a vine [Israel] out of Egypt; You drove out the [heathen] nations and planted it [in Canaan].*

9) *You prepared room before it, and it took deep root and it filled the land.*

10) *The mountains were covered with the shadow of it, and the boughs of it were like the great cedars [cedars of God].*

11) *[Israel] sent out its boughs to the [Mediterranean] Sea and its branches to the [Euphrates] River,*

12) *Why have You broken down its hedges and walls so that all who pass by pluck from its fruit?*

13) *The boar out of the wood wastes it and the wild beast of the field feeds on it.*

14) *Turn again, we beseech You, O God of hosts! Look down from heaven and see, visit, and have regard for this vine!*

15) *[Protect and maintain] the stock which Your right hand planted, and the branch (the son) that You have reared and made strong for Yourself.*

16) *They have burned it with fire, it is cut down: they perish at the rebuke of Your countenance.*

17) *Let Your had be upon the man of Your right hand, upon the son of man whom You have made strong for Yourself.*

18) *Then will we not depart from You; revive us (give us life) and we will call upon Your name.*

19) *Restore us, O Lord God of hosts; cause Your face to shine [in pleasure, approval, and favor on us] and we shall be saved!*

LETTER FROM PASTOR EARL

Greetings Covenant Family and Friends:

As Believing Believers in a Living Lord, we have the authority and power through prayer and fasting to change our lives, our families, our communities, our cities and yes, even world events. The events of our world, our nation, our economy and the crisis of our families, communities and cities demand that the Body of Christ maximize and utilize the weapons of our warfare.

Furthermore, the end-time purpose of God is the restoration of all things, especially His Great Church. Acts 2 and all of church history teaches us that the only source of power for this purpose is *desperate dependence upon the Holy Spirit and united prayer and fasting.* PAPA God is calling the Church to *"ARISE* [from the depression and prostration in which circumstances have kept you – rise to a new life]! *Shine* [be radiant with the glory of the Lord], *for your light has come, and the glory of the Lord has risen upon you! For behold darkness shall cover the earth, and dense darkness* [all people, but the Lord shall arise upon you O Jerusalem], *and His glory shall be seen on you."* (Isaiah 60:1, 2, AMP).

So, fasting and prayer will help you *"Lift up your eyes round about you and see!... Then you shall see and be radiant, and your heart shall thrill and tremble with joy* [at the glorious deliverance] *and be enlarged; because the abundant wealth of the* [Dead] *Sea shall be turned to you, unto you shall the nations come with their treasures."* (Isaiah 60:4a, 5 AMP). "The abundance of the sea"

> *...fasting and prayer can bring an outpouring of human resources.*

and "the wealth of the nations" are PAPA God's appointed provision of financial and technological resources to fulfill our great and final test on earth. And in the midst of the economic, emotional, plagued spiritual and relationship darkness – the simple yet supernatural tools of fasting and prayer can bring an outpouring of the human resources of Spirit-filled people and the material resources of wealth and technology.

Therefore, let us P.U.S.H until we See an outpouring of rain: *P*ray *U*ntil *S*omething *H*appens, Praise *U*ntil *S*omething *H*appens, and *P*ress *U*ntil *S*omething *H*appens. During this strategic 21 Day Daniel Fast with Prayer, Thanksgiving, Praise, Worship and Giving, according to Isaiah 58, you must Press into thanksgiving, praise and worship, Press into prayer, and PUSH AWAY from television and the wrong foods. For your fight of faith, memorize and speak against defeat with the following verses:

> [Not in your own strength] *for it is God who is all the while effectually at work in you* [energizing and creating in you the power and desire], *both to will and to work for His good pleasure and satisfaction and delight.* Philippians 2:13 (AMP)

> *I have strength for all things in Christ who empowers me* [I am ready for anything and equal to anything through Him who infuses inner strength into me; I am self-sufficient in Christ's sufficiency.] Philippians 4:13 (AMP)

With the help of Christ, the Holy Spirit – *YOU CAN DO IT! Drive and Go Forward! Because of Christ, we are...*

Freely Forgiven,
Pastor Earl

WHY THIS FAST, SPECIFICALLY?

I hear the voices of some saying "It doesn't take all that." And for those who say this, perhaps it doesn't for you and what you desire for you, your family, your community, your city, and your world. This I know – God is tired of our church celebrations that are all show and no substance. Listen to what He says:

> *"I can't stand your religious meetings. I'm fed up with your conferences and conventions. I want nothing to do with your religious projects, your pretentious slogans and goals. I'm sick of your fund-raising schemes, your public relations and image making. I've had all I can take of your noisy ego-music. When was the last time you sang to me? Do you know what I want? I want justice – oceans of it. I want fairness – rivers of it. That's what I want. That's all I want."* Amos 5:21-24 (THE MESSAGE)

Fervent and earnest fasting and prayer is the only tool to turn consumption with fashion to passion for God. The paradigm shift from entertainment celebrations to encounters with God demand that we seek God alone! And God Himself says:

> *"…and my people, my God-defined people, respond by humbling themselves, praying, seeking my presence, and turning their backs on their wicked lives, I'll be there ready for you: I'll listen from heaven, forgive their sins, and restore their land to health."* 2 Chronicles 7:14 (THE MESSAGE)

In my search of scripture, the most powerful spiritual tools to *"humble"* ourselves are sincere fasting and prayer. And when we dare to gather daily for thanksgiving, praise, worship and giving according to Isaiah 58, we launch a supersonic supernatural spiritual missile that breaks through the barriers of heaven preventing the release of *"showers of salvation gifts"* into our lives, families and communities.

HOW THIS JOURNEY WAS CONCEIVED?

In November – December 2007, during prayer I broke from a routine of kneeling to pray and started walking with my hands uplifted. One morning the Holy Spirit moved me to start crying out for rain. And when I started, sprinkles of rain fell on my arms. I asked myself, "how can spit get from my mouth to my outstretched arms?"

Then in late May, early June (2008), the Holy Spirit compelled me to more fervently pray for rain *"until"* there is a more tangible manifestation. When the Holy Spirit started to lead me to **"call this fast,"** everything in me fought it, especially the 6-9PM Daily Prayer, Thanksgiving, Praise, and Worship. Then during ALL-Night Unity Prayer on July 4, 2008, the sprinkling not only fell on me, but another person as well.

The third witness came while attending a Prayer Conference July 17-19, 2008. A worship group gave the testimony that while they were worshipping in Las Vegas (of all places) several months prior; it rained on a small area of the platform for one and a half hours. One of the worshippers stepped back into the rain and about a thousand people rushed to get near the rain. The rain wasn't coming from the roof through the ceiling – it started about one foot from the ceiling. This rain was supernatural rain. God is not prejudice – He will send an outpouring of rain if we **ask – knock – seek until it comes**! ASK the Lord for rain… (Zechariah 10:1a).

> *…we who are His servants and by our prayers put the Lord in remembrance of His promises.*

There are promises for this season that are unfilled. This fast was called to posture people in the third quarter of 2008 to be prepared for the muscle-building of the fourth quarter; because, just like in sports, how we play [fast, pray, praise and worship] in the third quarter can set the stage for the fourth quarter. God has promised that He is faithful and *"the Lord your God cares; the eyes of the Lord your God are always upon It [you] from the beginning of the year to the end of the year."* (Deut. 11:12, AMP). No matter what quarter of the year or life you find yourself in, this 21 Day Journey of Restoration and Transformation is a Holy Spirit inspired tool to build sinews, flesh, skin, and breath and spirit into the dry places of your life (see Ezekiel 37:6, AMP).

So, let us dare to go through this strategic Daniel Fast and be the watchmen upon the walls who will never hold their peace day or night; we who are His servants and by our prayers put the Lord in remembrance of His promises. Let us not be silent, let us *"Go through, go through the gates! Prepare the way for the people. Cast up, cast up the highway! Gather out the stones. Lift up a standard or ensign over and for the peoples."* (Isaiah 62:6, 10, AMP).

We will cast up or create the *"high way"* through our fasting, prayer, thanksgiving, praise and worship. The fasting and prayer will lead us to the praise and worship sound that unlocks the floodgates of heaven – with an outpouring of rain and salvation gifts.

LET US DRIVE AND GO FORWARD!

RESTORATION AND ASCENDING THE SEVEN MOUNTAINS

As I sat at my desk to write the Preface to this revised manual, the Holy Spirit said "Stop right now and read Daniel chapter one. Pay particular attention to the last part of the chapter and connect it back to the first part so that you can understand this 21 day journey and ascending the seven mountains." Please, permit me an aside for those with little or no familiarity with the "seven mountains" or "mind molders" to provide a very brief description here and call your attention to two must have resources: *Transformational Coaching* by Dr. Joseph Umidi and *The Seven Mountain Prophecy* by Johnny Enlow. In summary, "the seven mountains are kingdoms that shape the minds of men – they are the "mind molders" that form the culture and the spiritual climate of each nation. They are:

Church
Family
Education
Government and law
Media (includes all communication: TV, radio, newspaper, internet)
Arts, entertainment, sports
Commerce, science and technology

God spoke the following words to Loren Cunningham and Bill Bright on the same morning they were to have lunch: "If the world is to be won, these are the mountains that mold the culture and the minds of men. Whoever controls these mountains control the direction of the world and the harvest fields therein" (Umidi, 197). This is the *"season of the saints"* and like the four Hebrew boys, the saints must be mobilized. The sole paradigm of mobilization of the saints is to **S**upport them, **E**quip them, **E**ncourage them, and **R**elease them to ascend the heights of their assigned mountain. Yes, the prophetic clock of destiny demands a new breed of S.E.E.R. Pastor-Leaders who will not be content with "holy huddles" without calling plays that cause people to run the race of being *"salt and light"* that radically impacts the marketplace and the workplace. Daniel's purpose driven fast is vital to restoration that leads to the necessary empowerment to cause people to ascend the height of their assigned marketplace or workplace mountain.

> This is the "season of the saints" and the saints must be mobilized.

Now to the revelation, I believe, the Holy Spirit wanted me to receive and share with you. To prepare to receive this revelation, please read Daniel 1:17-20 prayerfully:

17) *God gave these four young men an unusual aptitude* **for understanding every aspect of literature and wisdom. And** *God gave Daniel the special ability* **to interpret the meanings of visions and dreams.**

18) *When the training period* **ordered by the king was completed the chief of staff brought all the young men to King Nebuchadnezzar.**

19) The king talked with them, and *no one impressed him* as much as Daniel, Hananiah, Mishael, and Azariah. *So they entered the royal service.*

20) *Whenever the king consulted them in any matter requiring wisdom and balanced judgment, he found them ten times more capable than any of the magicians and enchanters in his entire kingdom* (emphasis added).

In the past, I'd read Daniel chapter one on numerous occasions; however, I had *NEVER* connected the above four verses to the beginning of the chapter or to their powerful purpose driven fast. The beginning of the chapter shows us that Nebuchadnezzar gave very explicit instructions to his chief of staff "...to bring to the palace some of the young men of Judah's royal family and other noble families, who had been brought to Babylon as captives. Select only strong, healthy, and good-looking men, "he said' Make sure they are well versed in every branch of learning, are gifted with knowledge and good judgment, and are *suited to serve in the royal palace. Train* these young men *in the language and literature of Babylon"* (emphasis added). The chief of staff was instructed to get the *"Best of the best"* who were already qualified or *"suited to serve in the royal palace"*; however, the purpose driven fast of Daniel and his three friends caused them to exceed, excel, and ascend above all those chosen from the tribe of Judah as well as the magicians and enchanters of Babylon. In this season of the saints, PAPA God is requiring a remnant people who are *"already qualified"* by virtue of calling and destiny to commit to the purpose driven fast of Daniel as a process of repentance and restoration that leads to the global revival that He wants to see permeate every fabric of nations.

PAPA God is requiring a remnant people...

We are called to focus our ambitions and agendas upon bringing God's Kingdom rule into the fabric of cities, states, and yes, nations. We have been given the profound privilege to finish the task of receiving the inheritance of Christ. What is it you ask? Hear the Word of the Lord in Psalm 2:7, 8: "The king proclaims the Lord's decree. The Lord said to me, You are my Son. Today, I have become your Father. Only ask, and I will give you the nations as your inheritance, the whole earth as your possessions". Daniel and the young men were *trained in the language and literature of Babylon*. In this season of the saints PAPA God wants committed believing Believers to be trained in the language and literature of Babylon and more importantly the *"language and literature of the Holy Spirit."* Training in the language and literature of the Holy Spirit will empower you to walk in *"wisdom and balanced judgment"* and be *"found ten times more"* capable than lukewarm, Sunday go to meeting Christians and people who operate by the world's system. The language and literature of the Holy Spirit starts with understanding that the ***Kingdom of God is fourfold:***

The Principles of the Kingdom
The Patterns of the Kingdom
The Power of the Kingdom
The Person of the Kingdom

In Daniel's life we find the principle of no compromise and the pattern of the purpose driven fast to manifest radical restoration and transformation that created the rocket fuel for his ascension to the height of his assigned mountain.

This *season of the saints* is detailed as PAPA God has revealed it in Isaiah 59:19-60:5. However, in order to "see" the manifestation of these verses in a greater measure will require what Derek Prince calls an "enlargement of heart-an enlarged capacity to comprehend and to fulfill the purposes of God (157). This *21 Day Journey of Restoration and Transformation* can be used as a catalyst to the global impact prophesied by Isaiah because it meets the principle and pattern found in the book of Joel chapter two:

Existence of gross darkness (vv. 1-11)
A call and response to repentance through united prayer and fasting (vv. 12-17)
Restoration and renewed confidence in God (vv. 18-27)
Revival that leads to multitudes being saved and delivered: *radical transformation* **(vv. 28-32).**

PAPA God is waiting on His people to go through His process of repentance so that the resources that are reserved and set aside for the receiving of whole nations that will turn to Christ will be entrusted to us. He hungers to pour out the latter rain of His Holy Spirit and the rain of His Word in us, for us, and through us. *The Holy Spirit is the "Chief of Staff" of God's government.* Therefore, individuals, families, churches, and groups that embark upon this journey will experience radical restoration and transformation by the outpouring of the Holy Spirit who is the sevenfold spirit of Isaiah 11:2: "**And the** *Spirit of the Lord* **will rest on him – the Spirit of** *wisdom and understanding,* **the Spirit of** *counsel and might,* **the Spirit of** *the knowledge and the fear of the Lord*" **(emphasis added).** Dare to take the journey: Be restored, transformed, and receive the resources to ascend the height of your assigned mountain. *Hear the word of the Lord through the prophet Micah in chapter 4:1-4*:

> *...receive the resources to ascend the height of your assigned mountain.*

In the last days, the mountain of the Lord's house will be the highest of all – the most important place on earth. It will be raised above the other hills, and people from all over the world will stream there to worship. People from many nations will come and say, "Come, let us go up to the mountain of the LORD, to the house of Jacob's God. There he will teach us his ways, and we will walk in his paths." For the LORD'S teaching will go out from Zion his word will go out from Jerusalem. The Lord will mediate between peoples and will settle disputes between strong nations far away. They will hammer their swords into plowshares and their spears into pruning hooks. Nation will no longer fight against nation, nor train for war anymore. Everyone will live in peace and prosperity, enjoying their own grapevines and fig trees, for there will be nothing to fear. The Lord of Heaven's Armies has made this promise!

Like Daniel looked to *THE BOOK* and "...learned from reading the word of the Lord, as revealed to Jeremiah the prophet...." We must turn to *THE BOOK* so that we can see that it has been revealed to Zechariah that it is time to "Ask for rain in the time of the latter rain...." The principle and pattern outlined in *THE BOOK* is found in Joel chapter two. We must see that it has been revealed in *THE BOOK* that the prize we seek is the restoration of God's glorious church of Isaiah 59:19-60:5. Our source of power for this glorious task is united fasting and prayer.

GENERAL DANIEL FAST (OR ANY FAST) INSTRUCTIONS

Seven Guidelines for a Daniel Fast: These guidelines must be applied to any fast, for greatest results.

Guideline #1: *Be Specific* – In denying his desire to eat the king's meat, Daniel clearly defined his reason for objecting. Corporately, our stated purpose for this fast is *"for an outpouring of Holy Spirit rain and a rain of the Word that brings a God invasion of family and community restoration and transformation."*

However, personally what are you seeking God for? What specific area, circumstance, or situation that if you knew God would SHOW UP: you would go through the entire 21 day journey with passionate pursuit?

Write out your answer to the above question, make a commitment to the fast and sign it and date it! Hold on for the Spiritual ride of your life.

...what specific area, circumstance, or situation are you seeking God for?

_____

_____

_____

Signature_____ Date _____

Guideline #2: Fast as a commitment to seek God and don't be afraid to ask the Holy Spirit for guidance.

Guideline #3: Remember that *"Inner Desire"* is reflected in *"External Discipline"*.

a) During the fast you will reflect your spiritual commitment and DESIRE TO SEEK GOD by how much more you earnestly pray, praise and worship, and read the Word – slowly and reflectively. During this 21 Day Journey, you are asked to READ THROUGH THE GOSPEL OF JOHN, a chapter a day.

b) When you determine to fast for a specific time – keep the time commitment; don't let the devil tempt you on the door step of day twenty.

c) Faith is foundational to any fast! Your signed or spoken commitment to the fast is a statement of, A DECLARATION of, a DECREE of your faith. When the temptation gets tough, hold on to the truth of God's Word:

You shall also decide and decree a thing and it shall be established for you; and the light [of God's favor] shall shine upon your ways. Job 22:28

Faithful fasting will expose areas of your life God wants to kill. Remember, Paul said, *"I die daily."* (*I Corinthians 15:31*)

Guideline #4: A fast is an ideal time to pray and ask the Holy Spirit to *"Show you"* the role of sin in your life (e.g. health, relationships, finances, etc.)

> *Are any of you suffering hardships? You should pray. Are any of you happy? You should sing praises. Are any of you sick? You should call for the elders of the church to come and pray over you, anointing you with oil in the name of the Lord? Such a prayer offered in faith will heal the sick, and the Lord will make you well. And if you have committed any sins you will be forgiven. Confess your sins to each other and pray for each other so that you may be healed. The earnest prayer of a righteous person has great power and produces wonderful results. Elijah was as human as we are, and yet when he prayed earnestly that no rain would fall, none fell for three and a half years! Then when he prayed again, the sky sent down rain and the earth began to yield its crops.* James 5:13-18

> *Confess your sins to each other and pray for each other so that you may be healed. The earnest prayer of a righteous person has great power and produces wonderful results.*

In A Hunger for God John Piper makes this powerful statement: *"Fasting is God's testing ground – and healing ground.*

Guideline #5: Remember Daniel fasted as *a Declaration of faith* to others in the power of his God to MAKE A DISTINCTION. He and the other three "sons of Israel" would look better (shine, be light) at the end of ten days.

Guideline #6: Take the time of fasting to learn the foods that *"tempt"* you the most and "effects of foods on the body". Hint: The ones that tempt you the most are/maybe the ones God is saying aren't good for you.

Guideline #7: Surrender the results to God. Remember this mountain moving mantra God has given our church: When the *"WHAT"* is clear the *"HOW"* will appear. When the *"WHY"* is clear – you will have the power to persevere:

Your WHAT is clear – You want an outpouring of rain, not just on your life, your family, your church or your community.

Your WHY is clear – You want to see an invasion of God, you want to see His Kingdom invade earth, invade our churches, invade our families, invade our communities, and invade the nations of the earth. We settle for nothing less than a God invasion of restoration and transformation.

INSTRUCTIONS FOR UNITED/GROUP FAST

The previous guidelines also apply to the group or united fast. However, the following are vital guidelines specifically for united prayer and fasting.

First, *prepare the congregation or group before the journey.* No wise person takes a journey without proper preparation and a desire for a specific destination. Beyond the outpouring of the rain of the Holy Spirit and the rain of His word, what specific needs exist in your church, family, city, community, group, state or nation for which you are being compelled to fast and pray. *This is vital, because it serves to create agreement.* Recall that in Matthew 18:19 Jesus emphasized the supernatural power that is produced when believing Believers *"harmonize" "make a symphony"* or *"agree"* together in prayer. How much more supernatural power is released when the weapon of a fasting and prayer journey is taken.

> *No wise person takes a journey without proper preparation and a desire for a specific destination*

Second, *everyone taking the journey must commit to pray for "one another."* Remember, you become intimate with the One you pray to, the one you pray for, and the one you pray with. For this reason, *a family can be radically restored and transformed by taking this journey together.*

Third, *give the group or congregation clear instructions related to your context.* This manual is designed to take the overwhelming guesswork out of the journey and provide clear signposts. However, just as you want to provide specific needs to pray for –you must provide any specific instructions for your context.

Fourth, *identify a specific place and time where those on the journey will meet.*

Fifth, focus on prayer, thanksgiving, praise and worship. I am recommending this as a model; because, throughout Scripture these four go together like the ocean and water or whatever analogy you choose to use. I hope you get my point. Thanksgiving, praise and worship are necessary catalyst to the atmosphere of prayer. We cannot effectively communicate with Him until we enter His presence. So we *"Enter His gates with thanksgiving. And into His courts with praise. Be thankful and bless His name."* (Ps 100:4). Of course, it goes without saying that in His presence, the holy of holies – we worship. Remember, this is united prayer related to specific things so that we can be *"as one"* to *"make one sound."* So this, I believe, must be our passionate pursuit on this journey for any group:

> *"Indeed it came to pass, when the trumpeters and singers were as one, to make one sound to be heard in praising and thanking the Lord, and when they lifted up their voice with the trumpets and cymbals and instruments of music, and praised the Lord, saying: For He is good For His mercy endures forever, that the house, the house of the Lord, was filled with a cloud, so that the priests could not continue ministering because of the cloud; for the glory of the Lord filled the house of God."* 2 Chronicles 5:13, 14 (NKJV)

Paul and Silas didn't just pray – they prayed and sang hymns to God!

Sixth, *you must not expect everyone to attend every day,* especially for a congregational journey. However, for a family or small group, consideration must be given, beforehand, to the place, time, and amount of time to gather, to ensure maximum participation, every day.

Seventh, *teach and teach and teach the people on this journey to expect results.* WHY? God gave us permission to *"Ask for rain..."*, and *He promised to send the rain* (Zech. 10:1). Let me conclude this signpost on the journey with just two of many Scriptures that clearly show that PAPA God will respond with restoration and revival when we obey His principle and pattern of repentance found in Joel 2:12-17:

> *Now to Him Who, by (in consequence of) the [action of His] power that is at work within us, is able to [carry out His purpose and do superabundantly, far over and above all that we [dare] ask or think [infinitely beyond our highest prayers, desires, thoughts, hopes, or dreams].* **Ephesians 3:20 (AMP)**

> *And this is the confidence (the assurance, the privilege of boldness) which we have in Him: [we are sure] that if we ask anything (make any request) according to His will (in agreement with His own plan), He listens to and hears us. And if (since) we [positively] know that He listens to us in whatever we ask, we also know [with settled and absolute knowledge] that we have [granted us as our present possessions] the requests made of Him.* **1 John 5:14, 15 (AMP)**

...[we are sure] that if we ask anything (make any request) according to His will (in agreement with His own plan), He listens to and hears us.

FOODS TO EAT

Daniel primarily ate foods that were planted for harvest such as:

All Fruits: These can be fresh, frozen, dried, juiced or canned. Some examples of fruit are *apples*, apricots, *bananas*, blackberries, blueberries, boysenberries, *cantaloupe*, cherries, cranberries, figs, grapefruit, *grapes*, guava, honeydew melon, kiwi, lemons, limes, mangoes, nectarines, oranges, papayas, *peaches*, pears, pineapples, plums, prunes, *raisins*, raspberries, *strawberries*, tangelos, tangerines, *watermelon*.

All Vegetables: These can be fresh, frozen, dried, juiced or canned. Some examples of vegetables are to artichokes, *asparagus*, beets, *broccoli*, Brussels sprouts, *cabbage*, carrots, cauliflower, celery, chili peppers, *collard greens*, corn, *cucumbers*, eggplant, *garlic*, *ginger root*, kale, leeks, lettuce, mushrooms, *mustard greens*, okra, *onions*, parsley, *potatoes*, radishes, rutabagas, scallions, spinach, sprouts, squashes, *sweet potatoes*, *tomatoes*, turnips, watercress, yams, zucchini, veggie burgers, are an option if you are not allergic to soy.

All Whole Grains: For example, whole wheat, brown rice, millet, quinoa, oats, barley, grits, whole wheat pasta, whole wheat tortillas, rice cakes and popcorn.

All Nuts and Seeds: For example, sunflower seeds, cashews, peanuts, sesame. You can also have nut butters, including peanut butter.

All Legumes: These can be canned or dried. Some examples of legumes are dried beans, *pinto beans*, split peas, lentils, *black eyed peas*, kidney beans, black beans, cannellini beans and white beans.

All Quality Oils: For example, olive, canola, grape seed, peanut, and sesame.

Beverages: Spring water, distilled water or other pure waters; 100% juice with no sugar added, decaffeinated herbal teas.

Other: Tofu, soy products, vinegar, seasonings, salt, herbs and spices.

FOODS TO AVOID

All Meat and Animal Products: For example, beef, lamb, pork, poultry and fish.

All Dairy Products: Such as milk, cheese, cream, butter and eggs.

All Sweeteners: Such as, sugar, raw sugar, honey, syrups, molasses, and cane juice.

All Leavened Bread: Including Ezekiel Bread (it contains yeast and honey) and baked goods.

All Refined and Processed Food Products: For example, artificial flavorings, food additives, chemicals, white rice, white flour, and foods that contain artificial preservatives.

All Deep Fried Foods: Such as, potato chips, French fries, corn chips.

All Solid Fats: Including shortening, margarine, lard and foods high in fat.

Daniel committed to deny himself of the king's food. Amazingly, *"the King's food"* is connected to many of the health challenges that are taxing our healthcare system. What if God really is "up to something" when He said concerning "the right fast":

"Then shall your light break forth like the morning and your healing (your restoration and the power of a new life) shall spring forth speedily: your righteousness (your rightness, your justice and your right relationship with God) shall go before you [conducting you to peace and prosperity], and the glory of the Lord shall be your rear guard. Isaiah 58:8 (AMP)

Then shall your light break forth like the morning and your healing (your restoration and the power of a new life) shall spring forth speedily...

WHY PURSUE 3 OR MORE HOURS DAILY

FOR PRAYER, THANKSGIVING, PRAISE, AND WORSHIP

First, permit me to say that in my flesh, I struggle with this instruction as much as many of you may. However, I am settled in my spirit that this is something we MUST DO! Here I merely present just eight reasons why we MUST PRESS and PUSH to pursue 3 or more hours for prayer, thanksgiving, praise and worship. When you are unable to PRESS and PUSH your way to the House of God, you must PRESS and PUSH to pray, give thanks, praise and worship in your home. The eight reasons are as follows:

NUMBER ONE: When the Holy Spirit started to compel me with the intent and timing of this "Strategic Fast", He gave me the book of Joel, specifically chapter 2:11-32.

NUMBER TWO: In Joel 1, it says we MUST DO IT:

> *Announce a time of fasting; call the people together for a solemn meeting.*

Dress yourselves in burlap and weep you priests! Wail you who serve before the altar… Announce a time of fasting; call the people together for a solemn meeting. Bring the leaders and all the people of the land into the Temple of the Lord your God, and cry out to Him there. Joel 1:13a, 14

NUMBER THREE: In Joel 2, it also says,

Turn to me now, while there is time. Give me your hearts. Come with fasting, weeping, and mourning. Don't tear your clothing in your grief, but tear your hearts instead. Return to the Lord your God, for He is merciful and compassionate, Slow to get angry and filled with unfailing love. He is eager to relent and not punish. Who knows? Perhaps He will give you a reprieve, sending you a blessing instead of this curse. Perhaps you will be able to offer grain and wine to the Lord God as before . . . . Blow the ram's horn in Jerusalem! Announce a time of fasting; call the people together for a solemn meeting. Gather all the people – the elders, the children, and even the babies. Call the bridegroom from his quarters and the bride from her private room. Let the priests, who minister in the LORD'S presence, stand and weep between the entry room to the temple and the altar. Let them pray, "Spare your people, Lord! Don't let your special possession become an object of mockery. Don't let them become a joke for unbelieving foreigners who say, Has the God of Israel left them?" Then the LORD will pity His people and jealously guard the honor of the land. Joel 2:12, 13, 15-18

NUMBER FOUR: In Psalms 34, it says we MUST DO IT:

I will praise the Lord at all times. I will constantly speak His praises. . . Come, let us tell of the Lord's greatness; let us exalt His name together. Psalm 34:1, 3

NUMBER FIVE: In Psalms, it *SCREAMS* that we MUST DO IT:

Let this be recorded for future generations, so that a people not yet born will praise the Lord. Tell them the Lord looked down from His heavenly sanctuary. He looked down to earth from heaven to hear the groans of the prisoners, to release those condemned to die. And so the Lord's fame will be celebrated in Zion, His praises in Jerusalem, when multitudes gather together and kingdoms come to worship the Lord. Psalm 102:18-22

NUMBER SIX: The Principle of Kingdom Authority and Power demands that we MUST DO IT:

I tell you the truth, whatever you forbid on earth will be forbidden in heaven, and whatever you permit on earth will be permitted in heaven. I also tell you this: If two of you agree here on earth concerning anything you ask, my Father in heaven will do it for you. For where two or three gather together as my followers, I am there among them. (Matthew 18:18-20)

NUMBER SEVEN: The Pattern of the Early Church is our Model – So WE MUST DO IT:

They worshipped together at the Temple each day, met in homes for the Lord's Supper, and shared their meals with great joy and generosity – all the while praising God and enjoying the goodwill of all the people. And each day the Lord added to their fellowship those who were being saved. (Acts 2:46, 47)

NUMBER EIGHT: For me, this is the most important. The Word of God declares that it is not our name or the name of our church that is important; because anyone carrying His name MUST BE KNOWN AS A HOUSE OF PRAYER:

I will bring them to my holy mountain of Jerusalem and will fill them with joy in my house of prayer. I will accept their burnt offerings and sacrifices, because my Temple will be called a house of prayer for all nations. For the Sovereign LORD, who brings back the outcasts of Israel, says I will bring others, too, besides my people Israel. (Isaiah 56:7, 8)

LORD, SEND YOUR RAIN

THREE QUESTIONS TO DEFEAT TELEVISION/DVD TEMPTATION

There are three powerful questions that will challenge and encourage you to fast and trade the TV and DVD (other than praise and worship) for seeking God! No TV includes no Christian TV or Christians DVDs. Why?

The purpose of this fast is to seek the Lord, to seek an outpouring of His rain and His Word from Heaven, to acquaint ourselves with Him, now. To receive instruction from His mouth we must devote ourselves to personal and corporate prayer, thanksgiving, praise and worship. I know this will be greatly challenging to many of you, it will be somewhat to me as well. However, know that those who will fight through with faith will experience breakthroughs in your life and believe it will change your life and the life of your family for generations to come. God wants us to SEEK HIM!

By being a part of the Body of Christ in this season of your life – He, PAPA God has walked you to a pivotal crossroads in your life and your walk with Him. The following three questions are as important to your life right now as the two questions Jesus asked His disciples *"... Who do people say that the Son of Man is? ... But who do you say I am?"* (Matthew 16:13, 15). I beseech you by the mercy of God that you consider carefully your answer and your response. What do I mean? You can answer – nothing to all three and still allow the television to lure you the way satan attempted to tempt Jesus. However, if you really BELIEVE that the answer is NOTHING – you will be an OVERCOMER: LIKE JESUS! Just follow His example in Luke 4:1-14a. Just know that you are: 1) Filled with the Holy Spirit. 2) The Holy Spirit by this fast is leading you into a wilderness place, a barren area to test your dependence and trust in God and determine where the lust of the flesh, the lust of the eyes, and the pride of life still need to die in your life. The lust of the flesh, the lust of the eye, and the pride of life encompass the root system of all that satan has to offer; therefore, they are the root of any temptation he brings your way. 3) Like Jesus, you are determined to walk in the power of the Holy Spirit.

> *The lust of the flesh, the lust of the eye, and the pride of life are the root of any temptation satan brings your way.*

REMEMBER: there is no condemnation for those who belong to Christ Jesus" (*Romans 8:1*). However, this 21 day fast will expose the "greatness gap" in your life. It will show how much you say you love God versus how much you really love Him! Hear the Holy Spirit through the Apostle John in I John 2:15-17:

15) Do not love this world, nor the things it offers you, for when you love the world, you do not have the love of the Father in you.

16) For the world offers only a craving for physical pleasure, a craving for everything we see, and pride in our achievements and possessions. *These are not from the Father,* but are from the world.

17) And this world is fading away, along with everything that people crave. But anyone who does what pleases God will live forever (emphasis added).

Here are the three questions:

#1) What on television (or a DVD), even Christian, is more important than God Himself?

#2) What on television (or a DVD), even Christian, is more important than the rule and reign of God Himself, through the Holy Spirit in your life and your family now and generations to come?

#3) What on television (or a DVD), even Christian, is more important than finding and fulfilling God's Designed Destiny and Purpose for you on planet earth?

Don't let the devil defeat you – REMEMBER: He (God) has made everything beautiful in its time. *He also has planted eternity in men's hearts and minds* [a divinely implanted sense of purpose working through the ages which nothing under the sun but God alone can satisfy, yet so that men cannot find out what God has done from the beginning to the end (Ecclesiastes 3:11 AMP, emphasis added).

I promise you that the eternal treasure of Designed Destiny PAPA God has deposited in your heart is far more valuable than anything, including your favorite TV shows. If you won't accept my promise, then I pray you will accept your Heavenly Father's promise:

> *And I will give you the treasures of darkness and hidden riches of secret places that you may know that it is I, the Lord, the God of Israel, who calls you by your name.* (Isaiah 45:3)

Finally, please remember this fast is about seeking God for rain, not just for your church, for you, your family, or your needs and wants.

> *The clear focus is to see an outpouring of Holy Spirit rain and the rain of the Word that will result in a radical invasion...*

The clear focus is to see an outpouring of Holy Spirit rain and the rain of the Word that will result in a radical invasion of restoration for churches, families, neighborhoods, communities, cities and nations.

I BELIEVE IN YOU!

GOD BELIEVES IN YOU:

FAR-FAR-FAR MORE!

LET US DRIVE AND GO FORWARD AS ONE!

PERMEATE YOUR ATMOSPHERE WITH PRAISE AND WORSHIP

There are many who teach that united prayer and fasting should be devoted primarily to prayer; however, there are two reasons why this *21 Day Journey of Restoration and Transformation* must be bathed in and saturated with the atmosphere of thanksgiving, praise, and worship. This journey is about what we know God has already promised and wants to make a manifest reality in our lives, our families, our churches, our businesses, youth groups, etc. *Daniel knew what God was ready and wanted to do;* because, he *"…learned from reading the word of the Lord, as revealed to Jeremiah the prophet…"* (9:2a). Daniel knew that revelation demands involvement by an exercise of human faith and human will. Daniel understood the principle and pattern in the Word of God that PAPA God will never do anything that He has promised unless someone will dare to ask! For example, God through the prophet Ezekiel provided phenomenal promises in Ch. 36, even the promise of a supernatural new birth in verses 25-27. Still, in verse 37 **PAPA God demands human participation. "Thus says the Lord God: I will also let the house of Israel inquire of Me to do this for them: I will increase their men like a flock (NKJV).**

> ## *Daniel knew that revelation demands involvement...*

The principle and pattern that *we must ask* is threaded throughout Scripture and Jesus constantly discussed it throughout His ministry. He made it a major focus of His last discourse with His disciples. In each of the chapters containing that discourse we find the phrase "whatever you shall ask in My name":

> *And whatever you ask in my name, that I will do, that the Father may be glorified in the Son. If you ask anything in My name, I will do it.* **John 14:13, 14 (NKJV)**

> *If you abide in Me, and My words abide in you, you will ask what you desire, and it will be done for you.* **John 15:7 (NKJV)**

> *You did not choose Me, but I chose you and appointed you that you should go and bear fruit and that your fruit should remain, that whatever you ask the Father in My name He may give you.* **John 15:16 (NKJV)**

> *And in that day you will ask Me nothing. Most assuredly, I say to you, whatever you ask the Father in My name He will give you. Until now you have asked nothing in My name. Ask, and you will receive, that your joy may be full.* **John 16:23, 24 (NKJV)**

The above Scriptures prove the necessity of prayer. **The manifestation of prayer demands warfare.** Fasting is not only a form of self-humbling, mourning, or weeping-it is a strategic weapon of our warfare. One only need think about Jehoshaphat (2 Chronicles 20), Ezra in chapter eight, or Esther and the Jews in chapter four. **We must wage warfare to see the fulfillment of the prophetic promises and other answers to prayer.** Paul instructed Timothy to wage warfare *"…according to the prophecies previously made concerning you…"* (**1 Tim. 1:18**). Thanksgiving, praise and worship are mighty weapons of our warfare. For me, Psalm 149 clearly speaks to the idea that *thanksgiving, praise and worship are strategic warfare weapons:*

1) Praise the Lord! Sing to the Lord a new song, Sing his praises in the assembly of the faithful.

2) O Israel rejoice in your Maker. O people of Jerusalem, exult in your king.

3) Praise his name with dancing, accompanied by tambourine and harp.

4) For the Lord delights in his people; he crowns the humble with victory.

5) Let the faithful rejoice that he honors them. Let them sing for joy as they lie on their beds.

6) Let the praises of God be in their mouths, and a sharp sword in their hands...

7) to execute vengeance on the nations and punishment on the peoples,

8) to bind their kings with shackles and their leaders with iron chains,

9) to execute the judgment written against them. *This is the glorious privilege of his faithful ones.* Praise the Lord! (emphasis added)

Notice that verses 1-6 command us to use our human faith and human will to give thanks, praise and worship. Then, verses 7-9a tell us the primary purpose for our thanksgiving, praise, and worship. I believe that the Word of God clearly teaches that thanksgiving, praise, and worship is vital to united fasting and prayer, because *the enemy stations his greatest forces around our harvest.* And, the greatest harvest of the Christian Church is upon us! Jesus taught in John 14-16 that "we" "us" and "our" are far more important than "I" "me" and "mine." How? In all the whatever "ye" shall ask in My name passages, the "ye" is plural which is we, us, and our. We are the Church and Derek Prince provides the "...seven distinctive marks of the church at the close of this age:"

> *...worship is vital to united fasting and prayer.*

1) The church will be united in its faith.

2) The church will acknowledge Christ as its Head in every aspect of His person and work.

3) The church will be full-grown.

4) The completed church will present to the world a complete Christ.

5) The church will be permeated by God's glory.

6) The church will be holy.

7) The church will be without blemish." (Prince, 152)

These distinctive marks are why the gates of hell will seek to prevail against the fulfillment of the promises of God for you, for your family, your church, and your community. However, Jesus has promised that when we operate in wisdom with the principles, patterns, power, and person of the Kingdom of God: *"... the gates of Hades [hell] shall not prevail against it [His Church]"* (Matt. 16:18b, NKJV). The principle and pattern to prepare to wage war that breaks down the gates of hell is *the route of repentance, restoration, and revival* found in Joel 2. So this journey is about a *"united people"* waging warfare to:

"Go through, Go through the gates! Prepare the way for the people; Build up, Build up the highway! Take out the stones, Lift up a banner for the people" (Isaiah 62:10)!

Finally, thanksgiving, praise and worship are the fertilizer and water that causes the seed of our fasting and prayer to produce a harvest. This *21 Day Journey of Restoration and Transformation* starts with each individual. It is my firm belief based upon the Word of God that no person or group of persons can sincerely take this journey and step out of this God-orchestrated vehicle the same. Dr. Joseph Umidi wrote in the Foreword to my first book "...It is dangerous to read because it will ruin you for the ordinary. No longer will you or can you be satisfied with the artificial substitute." This *21 Day Journey of Restoration and Transformation* is dangerous to take because it will really, really, really ruin you for the ordinary. I state in a chapter entitled *"Kingdom Music Therapy"* that *"The only prescription for breaking free of the coldness of religiosity, the ritual of stale devotions, and the concrete of routine church attendance is to be a doer of the Word. I am convinced that daily, genuine worship and praise – in combination with the Word – is the crucial catalyst to create completeness in man's spirit, soul, and body (Brown, 131).* How much more can this be true on this *21 Day Journey of Restoration and Transformation.*

> **...fasting and prayer MUST be saturated with more time in the Word...**

Any expanded time of fasting and prayer *MUST be saturated with more time in the Word in such a way that the Word is "implanted" in our* hearts and become fruitful in our lives. Again, from *"Kingdom Music Therapy"* I quote from Jack Hayford's life–changing book *Worship His Majesty.* "The fruitful implanting of the Word of God is linked to our singing and worshipping... The complement of worshipful song is needed for the meat of the Word to be assimilated into our character and conduct. Just as our digestive system processes food and distributes nutrients throughout the body, so worshipful singing is apparently essential for the integration of the Word into our life (Brown 128). How much more will this implantation and integration of "...the Word into our life" accelerate during this *21 Day Journey of Restoration and Transformation.* So, as we embark on this journey let us declare with David in Psalm 138:

1) *I give you thanks,* O Lord, with all my heart; *I will sing your praises before the gods.*

2) *I bow before your holy Temple as I worship.* I praise your name for your unfailing love and faithfulness; for *your promises are backed by all the honor of your name.*

3) As soon as I pray you answer me; you *encourage me by giving me strength.*

4) *Every king in all the earth will thank you,* Lord, for all of them will hear your words.

5) Yes, they will sing about the Lord's ways, *for the glory of the Lord is very great.*

6) Though the Lord is great, *he cares for the humble,* but he keeps his distance from the proud.

7) *Though I am surrounded by troubles,* you will protect me from the anger of my enemies. You reach out your hand, and *the power of your right hand saves me.*

8) *The Lord will work out his plans for my life* – for your faithful love, O Lord, endures forever. *Don't abandon me, for you made me* (emphasis added).

RELEVANT RAIN SCRIPTURES TO BUILD YOUR FAITH

PRAY FOR RAIN
Holy Spirit – Send Your Rain

Old Testament

For the land which you go in to possess is not like the land of Egypt, from which you come out, where you sowed your seed and watered it with your feet laboriously as in a garden of vegetables. But the land which you enter to possess is a land of hills and valleys which drinks water of the rain of the heavens, A land for which the Lord your God cares; the eyes of the Lord your God are always upon it from the beginning of the year to the end of the year. And if you will diligently heed my commandments which I command you this day – to love the Lord your God and to serve Him with all your [mind and] heart and with your entire being – I will give the rain for your land in its season, the early rain and the latter rain, that you may gather in your grain, your new wine, and your oil. And I will give grass, grass in your fields, for your cattle, that you may eat and be full. Take heed to yourselves, lest your [minds and] heart be deceived and you turn aside and serve other gods and worship them, and the Lord's anger be kindled against you and He shut up the heavens so that there will be no rain and the land will not yield its fruit, and you perish quickly off the good land which the LORD gives you. *Deut. 11:10-15*

> *I will give the rain for your land in its season...*

If you will listen diligently to the voice of the Lord your God, being watchful to do all His commandments which I command you this day, the Lord your God will set you high above all the nations of the earth. And all these blessings shall come upon you and overtake you if you heed the voice of the Lord your God. Blessed shall you be in the city and blessed you shall be in the fields. Blessed shall be the fruit of your body and the fruit of your ground and the fruit of your beasts, the increase of your cattle and the young of your flock. Blessed shall be your basket and your kneading trough. Blessed shall you be when you come in and blessed shall you be when you go out. The Lord shall cause your enemies who rise up against you to be defeated before your face; they shall come out against you one way and flee before you seven ways. The Lord shall command the blessing upon you in your storehouse and in all that you undertake. And He will bless you in the land which the Lord your God gives you. The Lord will establish you as a people holy to Himself, as He has sworn to you, if you keep the commandments of the Lord your God and walk in His ways. And all people of the earth shall see that you are called by the name [and in the presence of] the Lord, and they shall be afraid of you. *And the Lord shall make you have a surplus of prosperity*, through the fruit of your body, of your livestock, and of your ground, in the land which the Lord swore to your fathers to give you. The Lord shall open to you His good treasury, the heavens, to give the rain of your land in its season and to bless all the work of your hands; and you shall lend to many nations, but you shall not borrow. And the Lord shall make you the head, and not the tail; and you shall be above only, and you shall not be beneath, if you heed the commandments of the Lord your God which I command you this day and are watchful to do them. *Deut. 28:1-13*

And Elijah said to Ahab, Go up, eat and drink, for there is the sound of abundance of rain. *Note: As the natural – so the spiritual* I King 18:41

When the heavens are shut up and there is no rain because your people have sinned against you, yet if they pray toward this place, confess your name [and you yourself] and turn from their sin when you afflict them, Then hear from heaven and forgive the sin of your servants, [all of] your people Israel, when you have taught them the good way in which they should walk. And send rain upon your land which you have given to your people for an inheritance. If there is famine in the land, if there is pestilence, blight, mildew, locust, or caterpillars, if their enemies besiege them in any of their cities, whatever plague or sickness there may be, Then whatever prayer or supplication any man or all of your people Israel shall make – each knowing his own affliction and his own sorrow and stretching out his hands toward this house – Then hear from heaven, your dwelling place, and forgive, and render to every man according to all his ways, whose heart you know, so you, you only, know men's hearts, that they may fear you and walk in your ways, as long as they live in the land which you gave to our fathers. *2 Chronicles 6:26-31*

Then He saw [wisdom] and declared it. Behold the reverential and worshipful fear of the Lord that is wisdom and to depart from evil is understanding.

From where then does wisdom come? And where is the place of understanding? It is hidden from the eyes of all living, and knowledge of it is withheld from the birds of the heavens. Abaddon (the place of destruction) and death say, we have [only] heard the report of it with our ears. God understands the way [to wisdom] and He knows the place of it [wisdom is with God alone]. For He looks to the ends of the earth and sees everything under the heavens. When He gave the wind weight or pressure and allotted the waters by measure, When He made a decree for the rain and a way for the lightning of the thunder, Then He saw [wisdom] and declared it. He established it, yes, and searched it out [for His own use, and He alone possesses it]. But to man He said, Behold the reverential and worshipful fear of the Lord that is wisdom and to depart from evil is understanding. *Job 28:20-28*

My root is spread out and open to the waters, and the dew lies all night upon my branch. My glory and honor are fresh in me [being constantly renewed], and my *bow* gains [ever] new strength in my hand. Men listened to me and waited and kept silence for my counsel. After I spoke, they did not speak again, and my speech dropped upon them [like a refreshing shower]. And they waited for me as for the rain, and they opened their mouths wide as for the spring rain. I smiled on them when they had no confidence, and their depression did not cast down the light of my countenance. I chose their way [for them] and sat as [their] chief, and dwelt like a king among his soldiers, like one who comforts mourners. *Job 29:19-25*

Who has prepared a channel for the torrents of rain, or a path for the thunderbolt, to cause it to rain on the uninhabited land [and] on the desert where no man lives, To satisfy the waste and desolate ground and to cause the tender grass to spring forth? Has the rain a father? Or who has begotten the drops of dew? *Job 38:25-28*

In the light of the King's countenance is life, and his favor is as a cloud bringing the spring rain. *Proverbs 16:15*

And now I will tell you what I will do to my vineyard: I will take away its hedge, and it shall be eaten and burned up; and I will break down its wall, and it shall be trodden down [by enemies]. And I will lay it waste; it shall not be pruned or cultivated, but there shall come up briers and thorns. I will also command the clouds that they rain no rain upon it. For the vineyard of the Lord of hosts is the house of Israel, and the men of Judah His pleasant planting [the plant of His delight]. And He looked for justice, but beheld, [He saw] oppression and bloodshed; [He looked] (for righteousness for uprightness and right standing with God), but behold [He heard] a cry [and distress]! Woe to those who join house to house [and by violently expelling the poorer occupants enclose large acreage] and join field to field until there is no place for others and you are made to dwell alone in the midst of the land! In my [Isaiah's] ears the Lord of Hosts said, of a truth many houses shall be desolate, even great and beautiful ones shall be without inhabitant. *Isaiah 5:5-9*

I will also command the clouds that they rain no rain upon it. For the vineyard of the Lord of hosts is the house of Israel, and the men of Judah His pleasant planting...

Therefore, the showers have been withheld and there has been no spring rain. Yet you have the brow of a prostitute; you refuse to be ashamed. *Jeremiah 3:3*

Yes, let us know (recognize, be acquainted with, and understand) Him; let us be zealous to know the Lord [to appreciate, give heed to, and cherish Him]. His going forth is prepared and certain as the dawn, and He will come to us as the [heavy rain] rain, as the latter rain that waters the earth. *Hosea 6:3*

Sow for yourselves according to righteousness (uprightness and right standing with God; reap according to mercy and lovingkindness. Break up your uncultivated ground, for it is time to seek the Lord, to inquire for and of Him. And to require His favor till He comes and teaches you righteousness and rains His righteous gift of salvation upon you. *Hosea 10:12*

Be glad then, you children of Zion, and rejoice in the Lord your God; for He Gives you the former or early rain in just measure and in righteousness, and He causes to come down for you the rain the former rain, the latter rain, as before. And the [threshing] floors shall be full of grain and the vats shall overflow with juice [of the grape] and oil.. And I will restore or replace for you the years that the locust has eaten – the hopping locust, the stripping locust, and the crawling locust, my great army which I sent among you. And you shall eat in plenty and be satisfied and praise the name of the Lord, your God, Who has dealt wondrously with you. And my people shall never be put to shame. And you shall know, understand, and realize that I am in the midst of Israel and that I the Lord am your God and there is none else. My people shall never be put to shame. And afterward I will pour out my spirit upon all flesh. And your sons and your daughters shall prophesy, your old men shall dream dreams, your young men shall see visions. Even upon the menservants and upon the maidservants in those days will I pour out My Spirit. *Joel 2:23-28*

Ask of the Lord rain in the time of the latter or spring rain and give men showers and grass to everyone in the field. For the teraphim (household idols) have spoken vanity (emptiness, falsity, and futility) and the diviners have seen a lie and the dreamers have told false dreams; they comfort in vain. Therefore the people go their way like sheep; they are afflicted and hurt because there is no shepherd. My anger is kindled against the shepherds [who are not true shepherds] and I will punish the goat leaders, for the Lord of hosts has visited His flock, the house of Judah and will make them as His beautiful and majestic horse in the battle. (*Ezekiel 34:1-10*). Out of Him [Judah] shall come forth the Cornerstone, out of Him the tent peg, out of him the battle bow, every ruler shall proceed from him *(Jeremiah 30:21)* And they shall be like mighty men treading down their enemies in the mire of the streets in the battle and they shall fight because the Lord is with them and the [oppressor's] riders on horses shall be confounded and put to shame. And I will strengthen the house of Joseph [Ephraim]. I will bring them back and cause them to dwell securely, for I have mercy, loving-kindness, and compassion for them. They shall be as though I had not cast them off, for I am the LORD their God, and I will hear them .... And I will strengthen [Israel] in the Lord and they shall walk up and down and glory in His name, says the LORD. *Zechariah 10:1-6, 12*

> *And it shall be that whoso of the families of the earth shall not go up to Jerusalem to worship the King, the Lord of hosts, upon them there shall be no rain, but there shall be the plague with which the Lord will smite the nations that go not up...*

And everyone who is left of all the nations which came against Jerusalem shall even go up from year to year to worship the King, the Lord of hosts, and to keep the Feast of Tabernacles or Booths. And it shall be that whoso of the families of the earth shall not go up to Jerusalem to worship the King, the Lord of hosts, upon them there shall be no rain. And if the family of Egypt does not go up to Jerusalem and present themselves, upon them shall be no rain, but there shall be the plague with which the Lord will smite the nations that go not up to keep the Feast of Tabernacles. This shall be the consequent punishment of the sin of all the nations that do not go up to keep the Feast of Tabernacles. In that day, there shall be [written] upon the [little] bells on the horses, HOLY TO THE LORD, and the pots in the LORD'S house shall be holy to the LORD like the bowls before the altar. Yes, every pot in all the houses of Jerusalem and in Judah shall be dedicated and holy to the Lord of hosts, and all who sacrifice may come and take of them and boil their sacrifices in them [and traders in such wares will no longer be seen at the temple]. And in that day there shall be no more a Canaanite [that is, any godless or unclean person, whether Jew or Gentile] in the house of the LORD of hosts (*Ephesians 2:19-22*). *Zechariah 14:16-21*

New Testament

But I tell you, love your enemies and pray for those who persecute you, (Proverbs 25:21, 22) To show that you are the children of your Father who is in heaven, for He makes His sun rise on the wicked and on the good, and makes the rain fall upon the upright and the wrongdoers [alike]. *Matthew 5:45*

Men, why are you doing this? We also are [only] human beings of nature like your own and we bring you good news (Gospel) that you should turn away from these foolish and vain things to the living God, who made the heaven and the earth and the sea and everything that they contain (*Exodus 20:11; Psalm 146:6*). In generations past He permitted all the nations to walk in their own ways; yet He did not neglect to leave some witness of Himself, for He did you good and [showed you] kindness and gave you rains from heaven and fruitful seasons, satisfying your hearts with nourishment and happiness. Even in [the light of] these words they with difficulty prevented the people from offering sacrifice to them. But some Jews arrived there from Antioch and Iconium; and having persuaded the people and won them over, they stoned Paul and [afterward] dragged him out of the town, thinking that he was dead. But the disciples formed a circle about him, and he got up and went back into the town; and on the morrow he went with Barnabas to Derbe. *Acts 14:15-20*

For it is impossible [to restore and bring again to repentance] those who have been once and for all enlightened, who have consciously tasted the heavenly gift and have become sharers of the Holy Spirit, and have felt how good the Word of God is and the mighty power of the age and world to come, if they then deviate from the faith and turn away from their allegiance – [it is impossible] to bring them back to repentance, for (because while, as long as) they nail upon the cross the Son of God afresh [as far as they are concerned[and are holding [Him] up to contempt and shame and public disgrace. For the soil which has drunk the rain that repeatedly falls upon it and produces vegetation useful to those for whose benefit it is cultivated partakes of a blessing from God. But if [that same soil] persistently bears thorns and thistles, it is considered worthless and near to being cursed, whose end is to be burned (*Genesis 3:17, 18*). Even though we speak this way, yet in your case, beloved, we are now firmly convinced of better things that are near to salvation and accompany it. For God is not unrighteous to forget or overlook your labor and the love which you have shown for His name's sake in ministering to the needs of the saints (His own consecrated people), as you still do. But we do [strongly and earnestly] desire for each of you to show the same diligence and sincerity [all the way through] in realizing and enjoying the full assurance and development of [your] hope until the end. In order that you may not grow disinterested and become [spiritual sluggards, but imitators, behaving as do those who through faith (by their leaning of the entire personality on God in Christ in absolute trust and confidence in His power, wisdom, and goodness), and by practice of patient endurance and waiting are [now] inheriting the promises. For when God made [His] promise to Abraham, He swore by Himself, since He had no one greater by whom to swear, saying, Blessing, I certainly will bless you and multiplying I will multiply you (*Genesis 22:16, 17*).... [Now we have this hope] as a sure and steadfast anchor of the soul [it cannot break down under whoever steps out upon it – a hope that reaches farther and enters into the very certainty of the presence] within the veil, (*Leviticus 16:2*) where Jesus has entered in for us [in advance], a forerunner having become a High Priest forever after the order [with the rank] of Melchizedek (*Psalm 110:4*). *Hebrews 6:4-14, 19-20*

So be patient, brethren [as you wait] till the coming of the Lord. See how the farmer waits expectantly, for the precious harvest from the land. [See how] He keeps up his patient [vigil] over it until it receives the early and late rains. So you also must be patient, Establish your hearts [strengthen and confirm them in the final certainty], for the coming of the Lord is very near! *James 5:7, 8*

> *For the soil which has drunk the rain that repeatedly falls upon it and produces vegetation useful to those for whose benefit it is cultivated partakes of a blessing from God.*

Confess to one another therefore your faults (your slips, your false steps, your offenses, your sins) and pray [also] for one another, that you may be healed and restored [to a spiritual tone of mind and heart].

Is anyone among you afflicted (ill-treated, suffering evil)? He should pray. Is anyone glad at heart? He should sing praise [to God]. Is anyone among you sick? He should call the church elders (the spiritual guides). And they should pray over him, anointing him with oil in the LORD's name. And the prayer [that is] of faith will save him who is sick and the LORD will restore him; and if he has committed sins, he will be forgiven. Confess to one another therefore your faults (your slips, your false steps, your offenses, your sins) and pray [also] for one another, that you may be healed and restored [to a spiritual tone of mind and heart]. The earnest (heartfelt, continued) prayer of a righteous man makes tremendous power available [dynamic in its working]. Elijah was a human being with a nature such as we have [with feelings, afflictions, and a constitution like ours]; and he prayed earnestly for it not to rain, and no rain fell for three years and six months. And [then] he prayed again and the heavens supplied rain and the land produced its crops [as usual]. *James 5:13-18*

All scriptures AMPLIFIED (emphasis added)

THANK YOU, GOD FOR YOUR RAIN!!!

WALKING THROUGH 21 DAYS

OF RESTORATION AND TRANSFORMATION POWER

When I was being challenged to write something to provide direction and structure for a 21 day Daniel fast, I believe the Holy Spirit directed me to write this manual and to use the Gospel of John. In fact, I was on the phone with the person the Holy Spirit used to keep challenging me when the idea, dropped in my spirit. Why?

The Holy Spirit may have more reasons; however, let me give you a few that come to mind:

1) The Gospel of John is one of the most important writings in the New Testament for a person who wants to walk as a Believing Believer. For me, the second is Paul's Letter to the Romans.

2) The Gospel of John brings the God of Genesis into our world. We are reminded that God spoke creation into existence and when we receive Him, we have the power to become the daughters and sons of God.

3) The Gospel of John declares that as sons and daughters of God, we have the authority and power through the "Right Use" of the "VOICE of OUR WORDS to CHANGE and TRANSFORM OUR WORLD.

4) *The Gospel of John presents the foundational TRUTH* that the Kingdom of God within us is entrusted to us for release in our homes, our social gatherings, the streets, the marketplace, the workplace and wherever we encounter hopeless and hurting people. How do we know? Jesus Christ performed His first recorded miracle at a wedding – who would have thought?

5) The Gospel of John contains, I believe, the three most important chapters in the Bible that instructs us on the most important person on planet earth – The Holy Spirit (Chapter 14-16). For me, the other three are I Corinthians 12-14.

The MESSAGE says "*The Word was first, the Word present to God, God present to the Word*. The Word was God, in readiness for God from Day one. Everything was created through Him; Nothing – not one thing! – came into being without him. What came into existence was Life, and *the Life was Light to live by*. The Life-Light blazed out of darkness; the darkness couldn't put it out... The Life-Light was the real thing: *Every person entering Life He brings into Light*.... He came to his own people, but they didn't want him. *But whoever did want him, who believed he was who he claimed and would do what he said, He made to be their true selves, their child-of-God selves*. These are the God-begotten... (emphasis added).

JOURNEY TO TRANSFORMATION QUESTIONS

1) Have you really received Jesus Christ? Do you really want Him?

2) Do you really believe that Jesus Christ is Who He says He is?

3) Do you really believe He will do what He said?

If you answered yes to all these questions...

Let the most transformational journey of your life

START TODAY!

DAY ONE

Read John Chapter One

POWER VERSES: Verses 1-5 and 10-14

POWER THOUGHT: The Christ who partnered with God in the creation of the world, now lives in me and partners with me by the Holy Spirit.

POWER PRAYER THOUGHT: Prayer is the voice that the enemy hates to hear.

POWER PRAYER: Father, I thank You today that Your Word was made flesh and lived among us. Father, I declare today that Your Word lives within me. Father, I pray for the boldness and sensitivity to the Spirit to release the authority and power of Your Word wherever I encounter hurting, hungry, hopeless, weary and wounded people. Father I declare today that as Your Spirit descended upon Jesus, the Rain of Your Spirit and the Rain of Your Word descends upon me as a fresh shower, as I faithfully fulfill this twenty-one day fasting and prayer commitment! I praise You and thank You in advance, in Jesus Name!

DAY TWO

Read John Chapter Two

POWER VERSES: Verses 5, 11, 21

POWER THOUGHT: When I obey whatever Christ instructs me to do I have the ability to bring God's future for me into my present. My body is the temple of the Kingdom of God.

POWER PRAYER THOUGHT: Prayer is the sound of wisdom in a confused world.

POWER PRAYER: Father, I thank You that You work in me by the power of Your Holy Spirit. I thank You that You have given me the will to take this twenty-one day journey with You! I declare today that You will also give me the ability, the power to faithfully fulfill this journey of transformation and I know that my life, my family, our church, and our communities will never, ever be the same again. Thank You Father, for teaching me to release the awesome power of signs, miracles and wonder working glory that resides on the inside of me.

DAY THREE

Read John Chapter Three

POWER VERSES: Verses 5-8, 16-18, 30

POWER THOUGHT: SHAZAAM! Just as I know I was born into a natural family, today I know I have been Born Again into the Family of God! WOW! WOW! WOW!

POWER PRAYER THOUGHT: Prayer is the divine report that contradicts all natural facts.

POWER PRAYER: Father, I thank You for my natural birth. Yes, Father I thank You for using my father and my mother to create my entrance into planet earth. Father I ask You today to search my heart to see if I am still holding any anger, bitterness, or unforgiveness toward my parents, myself or even You. Father I praise You for my new birth. I thank You for Your Precious Holy Spirit. Holy Spirit, just as the wind cannot be contained or understood, help me to stop trying to contain You or even understand You – Help me, Holy Spirit, to simply obey You even when I don't understand. Holy Spirit, as an act of my will, I give You permission to partner with me in the journey of life PAPA God has ordained for me. And I thank You that from this day – the Life-Light of Jesus Christ will shine brighter and brighter through my life.

††††

DAY FOUR

Read John Chapter Four

POWER VERSES: Verses 10, 13, 14, 21 24, 31-34

POWER THOUGHT: My primary purpose for existence on planet earth is to please and pleasure my Heavenly Father. Before my mother became pregnant with me – PAPA God had plans, purposes, and a Designed Destiny for my life: Finding and fulfilling them is the essence of "True Worship."

POWER PRAYER THOUGHT: Prayer is the revealer of God's secret purpose and plan for your life.

POWER PRAYER: Father, I declare today that I desire to live a life that demonstrates Your plans and purposes for my existence on planet earth. And Father, I admit that this act of *"True Worship"* is impossible without the help of Your Holy Spirit. Father, for this reason I have committed to this twenty-one day fast. In this fast, I say to You that I submit my body as a temple for Your Holy Spirit – a place for Your Spirit and Your Word to tabernacle. Father, I thank You in advance, I praise You in advance for an outpouring of fresh rain – Rain of Your Spirit and Rain of Your Word into every desert and dry place of my life and my family, by the Blood and Name of Your Son Jesus Christ.

DAY FIVE

Read John Chapter Five

POWER VERSES: Verses 5-9, 24-27, 30 34-36, 39, 43-47

POWER THOUGHT: When I surrender to the will of God for my life, His Divine Power will deal with even the deep-seated and lingering disorders of my life.

POWER PRAYER THOUGHT: Prayer is the Master Surgeon's silent instructor.

POWER PRAYER: Father, I thank You that Your Son Jesus Christ is the Divine Deliverer and the Divine Healer and He lives inside of me. Father, I thank You for new hope in my life and family. I recognize that hope is the mind's medicine, so I thank You for a healed and renewed mind today. Father I thank You that memory is the mind's method of motivation. So I thank You for the healing of my memories that have hindered me and I receive with Your rain the memory of the future You have planned and prepared for me. Father, I thank You that I recognize that focus is the mind's method of manifestation and as Your rain floods my life, I receive supernatural clarity and focus on Your prophetic destiny and promises for my life. I am a Worship Warrior with one strategic objective: To see the rain of Your Kingdom invade every arena of my sphere of influence – to Your Glory! So, today I cry out for rain, rain Holy Spirit. Holy Spirit, I need Your Rain! Holy Spirit, my family needs Your Rain! Holy Spirit, my co-workers and friends need Your Rain! Holy Spirit, send Your Rain!

DAY SIX

Read John Chapter Six

POWER VERSES: Verses 2, 15, 26-29, 35-40, 48-63

POWER PRAYER THOUGHT: When I make a commitment to intentionally make the Word o God more important than food and speak it boldly against anything I encounter that is no the will of God – the Words I speak will work the works of Christ, Hallelujah!,

POWER THOUGHT: Prayer is the bounty hunter of God's missing promises in your life.

POWER PRAYER: Father, forgive me for so often being like the crowd that followed You because of what they had seen or what they could or would receive. Please Father, I know in my heart that You and You alone are my greatest treasure. Forgive me for minimizing and taking Your Word for granted. Through this twenty-one day fast – restore me to a relationship with Your Word that is life-giving and permeated with miracle working power. Father, I declare today that I no longer do and toil for the food that decomposes and perishes – I passionately pursue the incorruptible, the indestructible, Word of God! Just as I was Born Again by Your Word, I now make a renewed commitment to live and walk by Your Word and by Your Spirit – every day of my life. HALLELUJAH! PRAISE THE LORD! THANK YOU JESUS!

DAY SEVEN

Read John Chapter Seven

POWER VERSES: Verses 8, 17, 18, 30, 37 -39

POWER THOUGHT: PAPA God by His Spirit wants to unlock the rivers of living water that are stuck inside my innermost being. When the rivers are unlocked, by the rain of the Holy Spirit and the Word, wherever I release the rivers everyone and everything shall be made fresh, be healed and live! GLORY! HALLELUJAH!

POWER PRAYER THOUGHT: Prayer is the key to God's power and presence. Prayer is the cosigner of the promises of God.

POWER PRAYER: Father forgive me for days, weeks, months, even years of stagnant and stunted growth. Yes, Father, forgive me for wasting so much of Your Precious commodity and gift of time. Father, I declare today that with the help of the Holy Spirit, I will redeem the time for the days are evil and people and situations are yearning for the manifestation of Your rivers – through my life. Father, I thank You that You are a God of Divine Acceleration so even though I may have staggered and struggled for twenty-eight years (however many for you), You PAPA are more than able and willing to activate Your Supersonic – Supernatural Rocket Booster of Divine Acceleration to walk me into Your Land of Promise for my life in twenty-eight months [however many months for you]. Father, I praise You In advance for Divine Supernatural favor and Divine Acceleration. PRAISE THE LORD! PRAISE THE LORD! HALLELUJAH!

DAY EIGHT

Read John Chapter Eight

POWER VERSES: Verses 1-11, 28-32, 42, 47, 51, 58

POWER THOUGHT: When I have a settled commitment to hear, receive and obey the Spirit of God and the Word of God, my life and family will manifest the will and Works of God.

POWER PRAYER THOUGHT: Prayer is Earth's commander under Heaven's authority. Prayer is the chauffeur in the valley of the shadow of death.

POWER PRAYER: Father, thank You for showing me how to be an encourager by Your interaction with the woman caught in adultery. Father, forgive me for the many times that I've hurt and wounded others with my words – as the men desired to stone the woman caught in adultery. Father, forgive me for so often using the creative power of my words to minister death to others rather than life. Help me, Holy Spirit! Help me, Holy Spirit! Help me, Holy Spirit to be an encourager, like Christ. No matter what people do, help me Holy Spirit to minister to them a corrective encouragement, a healing encouragement and the life-giving power of no limits encouragement. Father, I declare today that with the help of the Holy Spirit I walk with every person You've assigned to my life as a supporter and encourager of Your Destiny and Purpose for their lives. HALLELUJAH! PRAISE THE LORD! THANK YOU JESUS!

†††††††††

DAY NINE

Read John Chapter Nine

POWER VERSES: Verses 1-3, 11, 30-33, 39

POWER THOUGHT: Whatever happens in my life is divinely designed to give me the opportunity to display and illustrate to the unbelieving world the workings of God; however, heaven must hear my declaration of the will of God and "The Man Called Jesus' for my situation.

POWER PRAYER THOUGHT: Prayer is the prerequisite for divine supernatural release. Prayer is the weapon of mass destruction against the satanic kingdom.

POWER PRAYER: Father forgive me, for any doubt and unbelief that I've allowed to enter my life. Father, by the rain of Your Spirit and Your Word wash away doubt and unbelief and ignite the fire of faith that only You can give. Father, I thank You that You have promised me that I have faith; because You gave it to me as a free gift of Your grace! So, Father I declare that from today, I will use my faith, even though it only be the size of a mustard seed, to fulfill Your plans and purposes for me in my sphere of influence. Father, I acknowledge that You sent Christ to be a Separator and today I decide that I am fully enlisting in the army of God! I declare that I wear the uniform of *Ephesians 6:10-18* everyday for the rest of my life and I am covered with the blood of Your Son Jesus Christ. Father, I thank You that as a "good soldier" of Jesus Christ, with the help of the Holy Spirit, I march in step with Your destiny and purpose for my life and I never break rank; because, authority and submission to Your destiny is the most crucial weapon of my warfare. Father, thank You that I remain set, in position, to hear Your orders as I fast, pray, praise and worship, and devour Your Word! I thank You in advance for promotion and victory so that many nations will flow into Your kingdom, our church, and the churches of our city, county, state and nation. PRAISE THE LORD! HALLELUJAH!

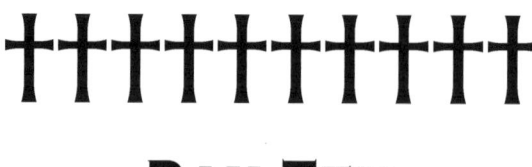

DAY TEN

Read John Chapter Ten

POWER VERSES: Verses 1-12, 25-30, 34-38

POWER THOUGHT: Because I carry the Spirit of God and the Word of God, like Christ, I am called to be God's representative on earth, in my sphere of influence. That is, through the Holy Spirit and the Word of God I can and MUST REPRESENT God to those I'm assigned!

POWER PRAYER THOUGHT: Prayer is the birthing tool, into the unknown, supernatural will of God. Prayer is the language that the entire world needs.

POWER PRAYER: Father, I know that I am Your sheep and that You call me by name. Please forgive me for permitting the thief and thieves to steal the finances and material possessions You prearranged and predetermined for me to possess and occupy. Father forgive me for permitting the enemies of my life to kill my health and allowing them to work with violent force to destroy the relationships that You have assigned to me in various seasons of my life. Father, today the tenth day of my commitment to You, I draw a boundary line with the Blood of Jesus in my life. Father, I declare that from this day things are placed in Divine Order in my life and I am an overcomer by the Blood of Jesus Christ and the Word of my testimony and I love, not the world, but I die daily to the influence of the world system. And I declare that no weapon formed against me shall prosper and every tongue that shall rise against me in judgment – I will condemn; because, this is my heritage as a blood bought, blood washed child of God. Father, I praise You in advance for helping me to grow from faith to faith, strength to strength, glory to glory so that I can shine brighter and brighter for You! HALLELUJAH! PRAISE THE LORD! THANK YOU JESUS!

✝✝✝✝✝✝✝✝✝✝✝

DAY ELEVEN

Read John Chapter Eleven

POWER VERSES: Verses 1-7, 14, 15, 25-26, 40-44

POWER THOUGHT: When Mary anointed Jesus' feet with perfume and wiped them with her hair it was *an act of warfare worship* – a seed to overcome death. I am a Kingdom-Carrier and when I make a commitment to wage warfare with worship, every dead person, situation and thing in my sphere of influence assigned to me must submit to the resurrection power of Jesus Christ.

POWER PRAYER THOUGHT: Prayer is God's tool of angelic instruction and direction. Prayer is a barricade against demonic attacks.

POWER PRAYER: Father, forgive me for any time in my life that I've permitted the death dealing enemies of inadequacy, insecurity and intimidation to cause me to draw back or give up on seeing Your perfect will for my life, my family and my sphere of influence. Father, with the help of the Holy Spirit, I want to know You in the power of Your resurrection. Father, I pray for the boldness to speak to the dead situations, the dead things and by the Spirit of Your Word – prophesy to the dry bones of people You place in my path so that they know You alone are God, King and Ruler of the universe. Father, with the help of the Holy Spirit, as I join my shout with my covenant brothers and sisters AS ONE, I thank You that we breakthrough the heavenlies. Thank You that You will flood the earth with rain and free people of their burial wrappings that have hindered them from being saved, serving You and waiting on You! Thank You in advance for Your resurrection power at work in me, for me, and through me – for Your Glory! PRAISE THE LORD! HALLELUJAH!

✝✝✝✝✝✝✝✝✝✝✝

DAY TWELVE

Read John Chapter Twelve

POWER VERSES: Verses 1-3, 20-28, 32, 44-50

POWER THOUGHT: As I passionately seek to serve and follow my Master, Jesus Christ as a living sacrifice, dying daily, receiving instructions from His mouth, and speaking His Word – *I release the Holy Spirit in my sphere of influence.*

POWER PRAYER THOUGHT: Prayer is the destroyer of premeditated disaster. Prayer is the advantage over every adversity.

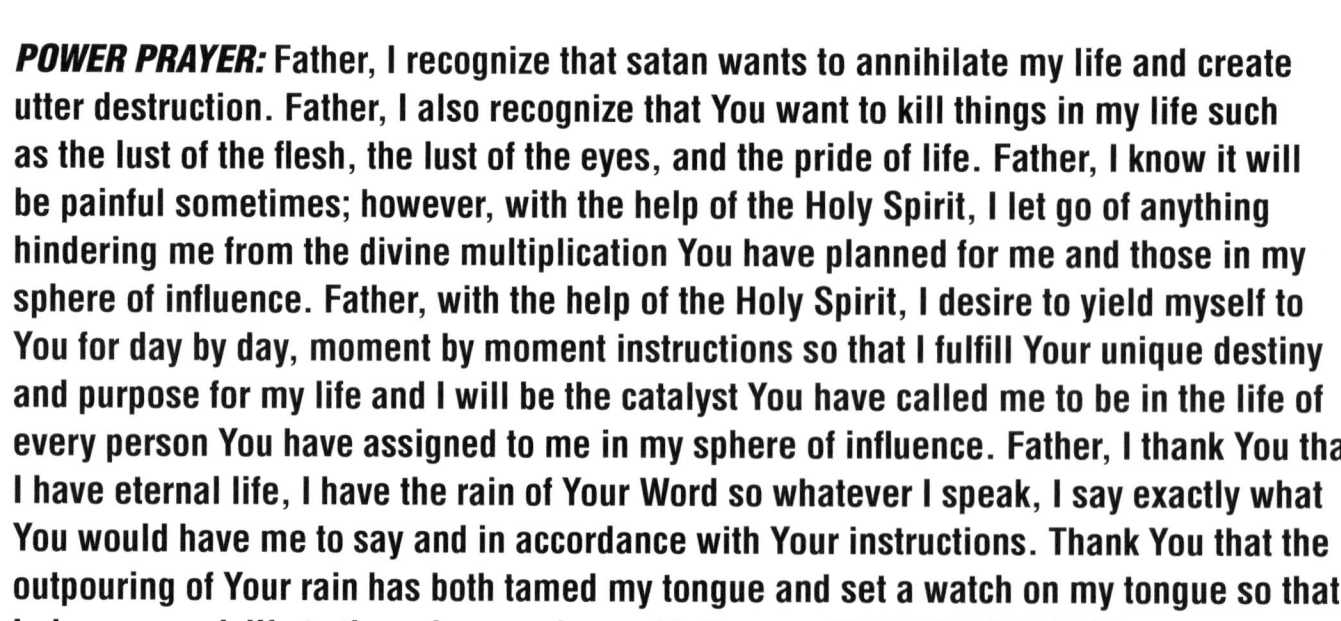

POWER PRAYER: Father, I recognize that satan wants to annihilate my life and create utter destruction. Father, I also recognize that You want to kill things in my life such as the lust of the flesh, the lust of the eyes, and the pride of life. Father, I know it will be painful sometimes; however, with the help of the Holy Spirit, I let go of anything hindering me from the divine multiplication You have planned for me and those in my sphere of influence. Father, with the help of the Holy Spirit, I desire to yield myself to You for day by day, moment by moment instructions so that I fulfill Your unique destiny and purpose for my life and I will be the catalyst You have called me to be in the life of every person You have assigned to me in my sphere of influence. Father, I thank You that I have eternal life, I have the rain of Your Word so whatever I speak, I say exactly what You would have me to say and in accordance with Your instructions. Thank You that the outpouring of Your rain has both tamed my tongue and set a watch on my tongue so that I always speak life to those in my sphere of influence. PRAISE THE LORD!

✝✝✝✝✝✝✝✝✝✝✝✝✝

DAY THIRTEEN

Read John Chapter Thirteen

POWER VERSES: Verses 1-5, 13-16, 31-35

POWER THOUGHT: Jesus modeled the "Mark of Christianity" for me by allowing Judas to participate in the covenant meal and washing his feet – knowing that Judas would betray Him. I can only have the power and strength to love as Christ commanded by the Holy Spirit.

POWER PRAYER THOUGHT: Prayer is the right reaction to satanic action. Prayer is the conqueror of satanic territory.

POWER PRAYER: Father, forgive me; because, I have so often betrayed You in so many little and big ways. I especially ask You to forgive me for failing to fulfill Your commandment in my own household and You have called me, no commanded me to love my enemies. Oh, God! I declare today that the level of love You have called me to is impossible for me – Please, Please, Pretty Please – Send Your Rain! Send Your rain! Send Your Rain! I don't want to be a closet Christian or a Sunday Church Christian, I want people in my sphere of influence to know that I have been with You. Father, I open my heart and life to an outpouring of the Rain of Your Holy Spirit and Your Word and I thank You in advance for a flood of rain in my life, my family and my sphere of influence. HALLELUJAH! PRAISE THE LORD! THANK YOU JESUS!

†††††††††††††

DAY FOURTEEN

For the next three days the Holy Spirit wants to stretch you beyond your comfort zone and force you to leave the land of familiar. How? Chapters 14-16 are best understood by reflectively reading them all at the same time, therefore...

Read John Chapters Fourteen – Sixteen (However, I will focus on power verses, one chapter at a time)

POWER VERSES: Verses 14:1-4, 6, 15-21, 23-31

POWER THOUGHT: Christ has NOT left me as an orphan – I have the Holy Spirit, the Great Comforter living in me. Yes, I have the Kingdom of God within me: God's righteousness, joy and peace.

POWER PRAYER THOUGHT: Prayer is the hearing aide of God to your spirit. Prayer is the mental silencer of emotional fear and torment.

POWER PRAYER: Father, I thank You that in the midst of chaos and turmoil, I have the Peace of God saturating my life. I thank You that You have NOT given me the spirit of fear. I praise You and give You glory that You have given me a spirit of power and of love and of a calm and well balanced mind and discipline and self-control. So, I thank You that in the midst of the instability of this world system; because, of the rain of Your Spirit and the rain of Your Word – I declare that I have rock solid stability of mind, will and emotions. By the help and power of the Holy Spirit, I will stop allowing myself to be agitated and disturbed, fearful and unsettled. I declare that I am more than a conqueror and that for Your Glory, I'm daring to take territory. Thank You that the Holy Spirit is in me, leading me and doing the heavy lifting. HALLELUJAH! PRAISE THE LORD! THANK YOU JESUS!

††††††††††††††

DAY FIFTEEN

Read John Chapters Fourteen – Sixteen

POWER VERSES: Verses 15:1-17

POWER THOUGHT: I am a fruit producing branch of the True Vine, Jesus Christ. What is so-o-o-o-o amazing is that He chose me to be His friend and fruit producer. *When I surrender to His purifying process He has given me the most phenomenal promise*: "…whatever I ask the Father in His name [presenting all that He is], He will give me what I ask"! I am a friend of God!

POWER PRAYER THOUGHT: Prayer is divine spiritual intimacy with God the Father.

POWER PRAYER: Father forgive me for failing to be an effective and maximized fruit producer. In *John 15,* You describe four categories of fruit producers, those who produce no fruit, some fruit, more fruit and much fruit. Father, in every area of my life I desire to be a *maximized much fruit producer* – to Your Glory. Father, I confess that without an outpouring of Your Spirit and Your Word I cannot have the desire of my heart to be a *maximized much fruit producer* to Your Glory. So, I have committed myself to this time of fasting, prayer, praise and worship, and giving with an expectation of a tangible outpouring of the rain of Your Holy Spirit and the rain of Your Word to invade every area of my life, my family, and my sphere of influence. Father, I thank You in advance, in Jesus Great name.

††††††††††††††††

DAY SIXTEEN

Read John Chapters Fourteen – Sixteen

POWER VERSES: Verses 16:5-15, 23, 26-27, 33

POWER THOUGHT: Christ died, rose again and took His blood to the mercy seat of heaven so that I could receive the Holy Spirit to be in close fellowship with me – to live in me. The Holy Spirit is my Comforter: Counselor, Helper, Advocate, Intercessor, Strengthener, and Standby. He partners with me and participates with me in all that PAPA God has designed and purposed for me to do.

POWER PRAYER THOUGHT: Prayer is the river that flows through "dry places." Prayer is Heaven's unlimited line of credit to Earth.

Unlimited ●—————● of $ >>>>> 🌎

POWER PRAYER: Father, forgive me for living my life as though You have left me alone. Lord Jesus, *forgive me for failing to take advantage of the Great Advantage You've given me by sending the Holy Spirit.* Holy Spirit, forgive me for having You in my house, my temple, and failing to fellowship with You and hold sweet communion with You. Holy Spirit, I declare today that You are the guarantee of my inheritance. You are the One who knows all the plans that PAPA God has for me. Holy Spirit, I declare today that You are the One that knows all of the treasures of darkness and hidden riches in secret places that PAPA God has deposited inside of me and in the earth for me. Holy Spirit I surrender myself to You, my Teacher, my Remembrancer, my Guide, my Revelator and the Great Administrator of my life. Holy Spirit, I thank You that You are the Spirit of wisdom; You are the Spirit of understanding; You are the Spirit of Counsel; You are the Spirit of might; You are the Spirit of Knowledge; You are the Spirit of the fear of the Lord: *YOU LIVE IN ME AND WALK IN ME*!!! HALLELUJAH! HALLELUJAH! HALLELUJAH!

✝✝✝✝✝✝✝✝✝✝✝✝✝✝✝

DAY SEVENTEEN

Read John Chapter Seventeen

POWER VERSES: Verses 20-26

POWER THOUGHT: I can live and walk with confidence that *Christ has prayed for me*, *Christ is praying for me* and *Christ will NEVER STOP praying for me*. When I struggle with having confidence in my prayers – I can stand firm in the fact that *Christ prays His Word for me and the Father always hears Him.*

POWER PRAYER THOUGHT: Prayer is your promised potential. Prayer is one of the greatest supports of obedience to God.

POWER PRAYER: Father, I thank You for sending Your Son, Jesus Christ to die for me. Father, I thank You for the Great love You demonstrated. Lord Jesus, I thank You that in Your High Priestly Prayer You showed me the importance of *praying for myself, for all those in my present sphere of influence* as well as *generations to come*. Father, forgive me for failing to be intentional about allowing the Holy Spirit to create oneness in my home, in my local congregation, and among the local congregations of my city. Father, I know that an outpouring of the rain of Your Holy Spirit along with an outpouring of the rain of Your Word will produce the level of unity You desire and the quality of unity that will create the new smell, the new scent that You have declared for the City of Lakeland [your City]. Father, send Your Rain, Send Your Rain, We Need Your Rain!

✝✝✝✝✝✝✝✝✝✝✝✝✝✝✝✝

DAY EIGHTEEN

Read John Chapter Eighteen

POWER VERSES: Verses 5, 6, 11, 36-37

POWER THOUGHT: Whenever I declare "*I am*" anything – I am strong, I am rich, I am healed, I am healthy, I am more than a conqueror: It is backed and supported by the Great *I AM*! I am in the world, but not of the world because *I live out of the resources of the Kingdom of God that is within me.*

POWER PRAYER THOUGHT: Prayer is the invisible locksmith to closed doors. Prayer is therapy for a crippled spirit.

POWER PRAYER: Father, I thank You that the Kingdom of God is within me. Father, I thank You that You are the God of my hope and You fill me with all joy and peace in believing by the power of the Holy Spirit. I abound, I overflow, and bubble over with hope! Father, I praise You that when You could swear by no other, You swore by Yourself. I declare today that I hold fast my hope in You; because it is impossible for You to ever be proven false or deceive. I declare that I have You as my hope as a sure and steadfast anchor of the soul – it cannot slip and it cannot break down under whoever steps out upon it. So, nothing can ever separate me from Your love and Your promises for my life, my family, and those You have assigned to me in my sphere of influence. So, Father I thank You in advance for a mighty outpouring of Your Holy Spirit rain and a flood of the rain of Your Word! In Jesus Great Name and by His Blood! HALLELUHAH!

†††††††††††††††††††††

DAY NINETEEN

Read John Chapter Nineteen

POWER VERSES: Verses 4, 6, 10-15, 25-30, 38-42

POWER THOUGHT: When Christ declared from the cross – "*It is finished*" He set the stage for me to choose to be a part of the family of God, experience *the freedom of being freely forgiven*, the *freedom to seek and find my identity* in God and Christ alone so that I can *live the Designed Destiny He prepared for me* before the foundations of the earth.

POWER PRAYER THOUGHT: Prayer is the heavenly commander over the army that is waiting above your head. Prayer is the destroyer of premeditated disorder.

POWER PRAYER: Father, forgive me for sometimes living my life as though I have no king but Caesar! Father, help me by the power and presence of Your Holy Spirit to *with utter abandon*, seek Your Kingdom and Your righteousness above any and everything else in my life. Father, send Your precious rain of restoration and transformation to flood and invade every area of my life. Yes, restore me again, O God; and cause Your face to shine in pleasure and approval on me and I shall never betray You. Restore me again, O God of Hosts; and cause Your face to shine upon me with favor as of old and I shall be saved. Yes, O Lord God of Hosts; cause Your face to shine in pleasure, approval, and favor on me and I shall be saved! Turn again, I cry out to You, O God of Hosts! Look down from heaven and see, visit, and have regard for this vine! Rain on me! Rain on my family! Rain on my assignment and my sphere of influence. Yes, Father, have pity and spare Your people, O Lord and give not Your heritage to reproach that the heathen nations should rule over us or use a byword against us. Why, Father should they say among the people, where is our God? So, Rain on us, send an outpouring of the rain of Your Holy Spirit and the rain of Your Word.

††††††††††††††††††††††

DAY TWENTY

Read John Chapter Twenty

POWER VERSES: Verses 8-10, 15-23. 26-29

POWER THOUGHT: As PAPA God sent Christ, He has sent me by and through the power of the Holy Spirit. I have the authority to release people or hold them hostage by failing to forgive. With the help of the Holy Spirit, I don't need to see to believe – *I believe to see the goodness of the Lord in the land of the living.*

POWER PRAYER THOUGHT: Prayer is the initiator of an angelic obligation. Prayer is the designated driver of my destiny.

POWER PRAYER: Father, forgive me for so very often being like "the other disciple" and Thomas – having a need to see, to be convinced and believe. Father, I know that You desire that I live and walk by faith and not by sight. However, Father I must acknowledge that without a continued shower of the rain of Your Holy Spirit and the rain of Your Word, I'll be like Peter before Pentecost. Father, I desire to be a witness for You and never put You to shame. So, Father I cry out to You for an outpouring of Your Holy Spirit rain and a flood of Your Word as the waters cover the sea. Your Word is spirit and life. Shower me, shower my family, shower my sphere of influence with your active, energizing, soul penetrating and heart reading Word, in the name of Your Son Jesus and by His Blood. I thank You in advance and I praise You in advance.

†††††††††††††††††††††††

DAY TWENTY-ONE

Read John Chapter Twenty-One

POWER VERSES: Verses 5-19

POWER THOUGHT: Though I may struggle and attempt to go back to my old life – the love of Christ will come seeking me with the cry: *Come and dine!*

POWER PRAYER THOUGHT: Prayer is the locator of Your most wanted list of hidden promises. Prayer is the agent of increase in an economic famine.

POWER PRAYER: Father forgive me for the times I've struggled. Forgive me for the times I've failed to obey Your instructions or obeyed, but did it on my time table and not Yours. Father, with the help of the Holy Spirit, I pray that I will always move and operate on the basis of faith and not sight. Help me to stay in the Word of God so that my faith can grow exceedingly. Father, I take the authority You have given me and I command every mountain I am facing to bow to the Word of God. I declare that the things I am hoping for will surely come to pass. I thank You that this fast has increased my faith and my intimate fellowship with You! I thank You that the entrance of Your Word over these twenty-one days has produced greater growth and maturity in my life. Father, *I pray that my faith, the fresh outpouring of Your Holy Spirit and Your Word will produce an ever-increasing flow of spiritual, emotional, physical, relationship, and financial prosperity in my life.* And Father, I thank You in advance, I shout in advance, I dance in advance; because, I know You are faithful to fulfill Your Word!

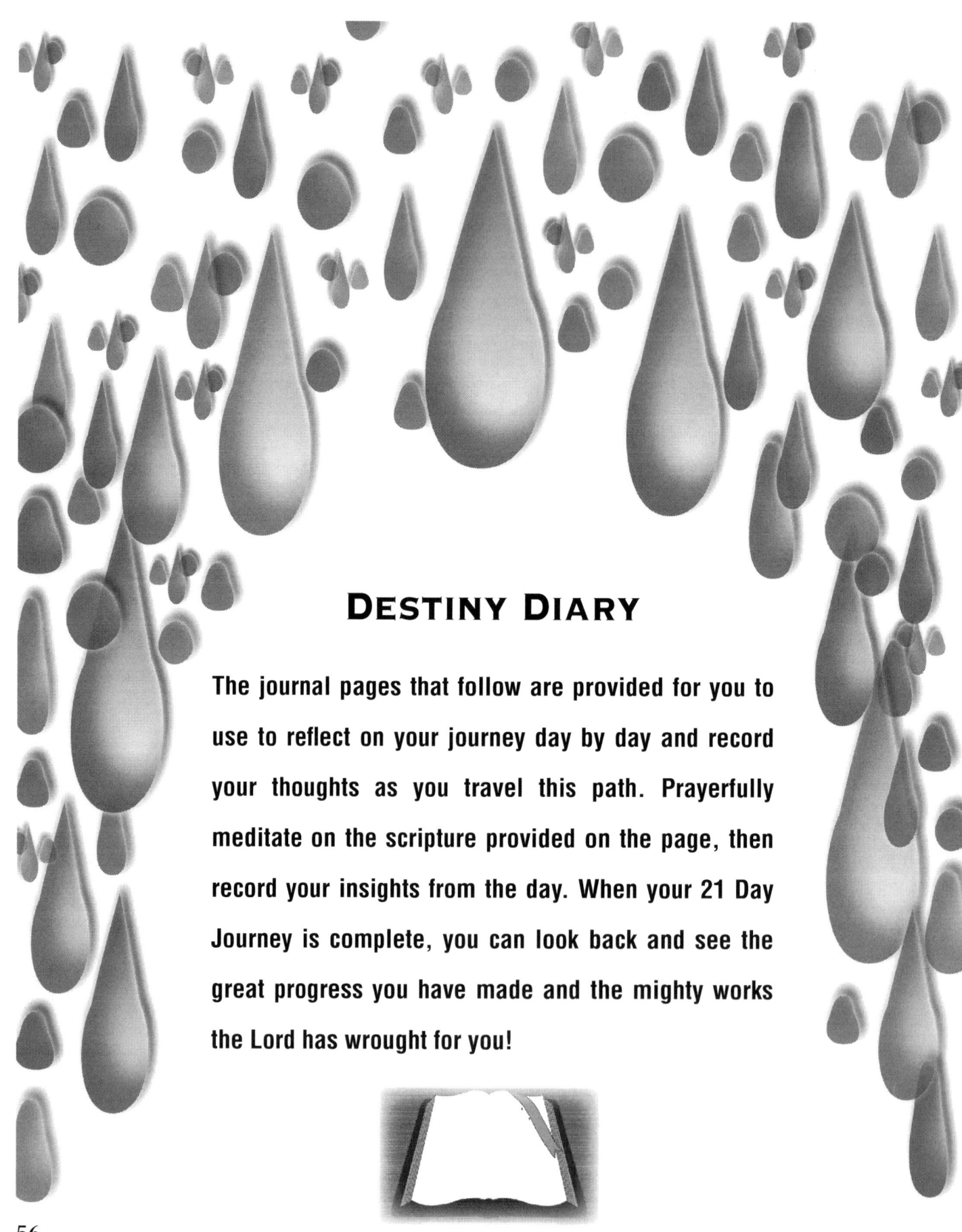

DESTINY DIARY

The journal pages that follow are provided for you to use to reflect on your journey day by day and record your thoughts as you travel this path. Prayerfully meditate on the scripture provided on the page, then record your insights from the day. When your 21 Day Journey is complete, you can look back and see the great progress you have made and the mighty works the Lord has wrought for you!

DAY ONE

Lord, hear my prayer! Listen to my plea! (Psalm 102:1)

57

DAY TWO

Enter his gates with thanksgiving, go into his courts with praise.
Give thanks to him and praise his name. (Psalm 100:4)

DAY THREE

DAY FOUR

Send me a sign of your favor...for you, O Lord, help and comfort me. (Psalm 86:17)

DAY FIVE

DAY SIX

He will show them the path they should choose. (Psalm 25:12b)

DAY SEVEN

DAY EIGHT

Let your favor shine on your servant. In your unfailing love, rescue me. (Psalm 31:16)

DAY NINE

DAY TEN

Yes, ask me for anything in my name, and I will do it! (John 14:14)

DAY ELEVEN

When the Spirit of truth comes,...He will tell you about the future. (John 16:13)

DAY TWELVE

Don't let your hearts be troubled. Trust in God, and trust also in me. (John 14:1)

DAY THIRTEEN

DAY FOURTEEN

Commit everything you do to the Lord. Trust him, and he will help you. (Psalm 37:5)

DAY FIFTEEN

Be still and know that I am God! I will be honored by every nation.
I will be honored throughout the world. (Psalm 46:10)

71

DAY SIXTEEN

...You are my Father, my God, and the Rock of my salvation. (Psalm 89:26b)

DAY SEVENTEEN

As soon as I pray, you answer me; you encourage me by giving me strength. (Psalm 138:3)

DAY EIGHTEEN

Let every created thing give praise to the Lord, for he issued his command, and they came into being. (Psalm 148:5)

DAY NINETEEN

Praise his name with dancing,.....
Let the praises of God be in their mouths.... (Psalm 149:3a, 6a)

DAY TWENTY

For I know the plans I have for you says the Lord...
to give you a future and a hope. (Jeremiah 29:11)

DAY TWENTY-ONE

Arise...! Let your light shine for all to see.
For the glory of the Lord rises to shine on you. (Isaiah 60:1)

BIBLIOGRAPHY

Ashimolowo, Matthew A., *The Positive Power of Prayer*, Special Anniversary Edition, Volume 1,2,& 3, Matthew Ashimolowo Media Ministries, P.O. Box 12961, London E15 1UR, 1998

Brown, R. Earl, Help Me God! I Still Yearn for My Earthly Father's Affection. Xulon Press: Longwood, FL 2004.

Enlow, Johnny, *The Seven Mountain Prophecy*, Creation House: Lake Mary, FL 2008.

Hayford, Jack W. Worship His Majesty: How Praising the King of Kings Will Change your Life. WORD Publishing: Dallas, TX, 1987

McKnight, Jonathan L., Prayer is a Must: A Spiritual Handbook to Prevail in Prayer, JLM Publishing: Orlando, FL, 2008.

Piper, John, A Hunger for God: Desiring God Through Fasting and Prayer, Crossway Books: Wheaton, IL, 1997.

Prince, Derek, *Shaping History Through Prayer & Fasting*, Derek Prince Ministries: Charlotte, NC, 1973.

Strong, James, LL.D., S.T.D., *THE NEW STRONG'S EXHAUSTIVE CONCORDANCE OF THE BIBLE,* Thomas Nelson Publishers: Nashville: TN, 1990.

Towns, Elmer L., *Fasting for Spiritual Breakthrough,* Gospel Light Publications: Ventura, CA, 1996.

Umidi, Joseph Dr., Transformational Coaching: Bridge Building that Impacts, Connects, and Advances the Ministry and the Marketplace, Xulon Press: Longwood, FL, 2005.

PRODUCT ORDER FORM

BOOKS & CDS

_____ 21 Day Journey of Restoration & Transformation $15.00

_____ 21–Day Journey: Power Prayer and Thought (CD) .... $ 7.00
PLUS: One free CD from Pastor Letitia Stones' Call of the Kingdom series!

_____ 21–Day Journey: Prayerful Moments Instrumental (CD) .... $ 12.00
This anointed instrumental music track from the Power Prayer and Thought CD was composed by renowned worshiper Valerie R. Harris. For information, visit www.leviticalvessels.org or contact her at: Levitical Vessels, P.O. Box 367, Trussville, AL 35173, valerieharris@leviticalvessels.org

_____ Help Me God! I Still Yearn for... Father's Affection – Earl Brown $13.00

_____ Transformational Coaching – Dr. Joseph Umidi $20.00

_____ The Call of the Kingdom: Intimacy-Inner Strength-Impact (4 CDs) $23.95
Anointed series by Pastor Letitia Stones

_____ I Lived To Tell About It – Pastor Joey Perez $17.00

_____ True Prayer Produces True Prosperity:
God's Roadmap to Become a Kingdom Distributor of Wealth $29.95

_____ Per title shipping & handling $3.00

TRAININGS/WORKSHOPS/SEMINARS

_____ How to Uncover & Live Your Destiny

_____ PREPARE/ENRICH (Premarital/Marriage Enrichment Training)

_____ PAIRS™ (Marriage Enrichment Workshop)

_____ Jumpstart – Family Wellness – Interactive Training For Families

_____ The ACT Program (Accelerated Coach Training)

_____ Real Talk (One-day Seminar in Interpersonal Communication)

Visit our coach training web site at www.hopecoaching.org

Name _____

Address _____

City _____ ST _____ Zip _____

Method of Payment: _____Cash _____ Check _____ Money Order _____Credit Card

Credit Card # _____

Type: _____ MasterCard _____ Visa   Exp. Date: Month/Year_____

Name as it appears on card _____

RECOMMENDED RESOURCES

PRAISE & WORSHIP

First and foremost, use what works for you. However, during this journey join in and sing along and dance! God created dancing – not the devil. The devil is a distorter, distracter and deceiver! Besides, one of the definitions of *"travail"* is to dance, to twist, to twirl. Dare to dance your way into restoration, transformation and birthing people into the kingdom!

Binion, David & Nicole and friends, *"The Sound of Heaven"*, Volume 1, 2003, www.thesoundofheaven.com, davenicole611@aol.com, 904-642-3220. For this 21 Day Journey, tracks 7-13 on Disc 2 – Pray For Rain (Reprise) and Rain Dance are absolutely phenomenal!

Brooklyn Tabernacle Choir, *"I'll Say Yes"*, 2008, Brooklyn Tabernacle Church, www.IntegrityMusic.com/TheBrooklynTabernacleChoir. For me, absolutely **anything** by the Brooklyn Tabernacle Choir will help to make this 21 Day Journey more restorative and transformative. **I really do mean anything!** When our children were still at home, we fast the television for 18 months and primarily watched Brooklyn Tabernacle videos.

Dixon, Ronnie, *"Ronnie's Amazing"*. This two song CD will bless your life because it is the soulful and pure sound of a young man who hungers for the heart of God! Join him as he prays in song – "Let it rain!" He was also hand-picked by me and my wife to sing on a recording with her entitled *"I Still Want My Father's Love"*, which you can obtain through Giving People Hope, P.O. Box 92893, Lakeland, Florida 33804-2893 or www.hopecoaching.org.

Garlington, Joseph, *"Live Worship"*, 2002, Recorded Live at Covenant Church of Pittsburg, www.ccop.org or call 412-731-7887. To me, Bishop Garlington's life and ministry demonstrates *"true worship."* Therefore, you will receive an impartation during your journey. I would recommend any of his praise and worship music.

...truly words to this generation and generations to come!

Israel & New Breed, *"Deeper Level"*, 2007 Integrity Media, www.IntegrityMusic.com, www.NewBreedMusic.com. I've never heard an Israel & New Breed CD that didn't have "loads" of songs that touched my heart; however, on this CD *"Identity"*, *"I Know Who I Am"* and *"If Not For Your Grace"*, are truly words to this generation and generations to come! To pursue this journey with intensity and sincerity and soak oneself in those three songs, I believe, will accelerate personal restoration and transformation.

Jacobs, Judy, *"Almighty Reigns"*, 2005, His Song Music Group: Cleveland, TN, product@judyjacobs.com, www.judyjacobs.com. I am a word "WARRIOR". When I first heard the first song on this powerful CD, I said *"this woman is a warrior."* Her warrior anointing and spirit will open your heart, help build your faith, and be a catalytic converter to your journey of restoration and transformation.

Lawrence, Antonia, *"Free to Be Me"*, 2002, 1st Commandment Publishing, www.antonialawrence.com. I was introduced to Antonia's ministry by my late spiritual friend and mentor, Bishop Val Melendez in 1998. He said "I had to meet David Lawrence and his wife Antonia." He was right! Antonia's pureness of worship will catapult you to restoration and transformation. My favorite is *"Butterfly (Free To Be Me)."* And of course for this journey *"Let It Rain."*

Munizzi, Martha, *"Change the World"*, 2008, Central South Distribution, Nashville, TN, www.marthamunizzi.com. We are called to *"Change the World."* So, when we know that we are His *"Habitation"* we can *"Dance"*; because, we know that He is *"More Than Enough"* and His *"Favor"* will flood our lives to fulfill His assignments! Need I say more. Get it, and get upon your feet and dance your way to restoration and transformation.

Munizzi, Martha, *"No Limits"*, 2006, Integrity Music, Mobile, AL, same web site as above. Both Discs are powerful; however, my favorite is Disc 2, especially the first three songs that are melodies of invitation and prayer to the Holy Spirit.

Sapp, Marvin, *"Thirsty"*, 2007, Somba Recording LLC, Song BMG Music, www.marvinsapp.com, www.lighthouseflc.com. Personally, I struggle with some of the music on this CD; however, the struggle is worth it for the warfare praise of *"Possess the Land"* and *"Praise Him in Advance."* Your desire to take this journey must be because you are *"Thirsty"* and there is a yearning to see your *"Rivers Flow."* And of course, by the time you finish the journey you'll be saying over and over again, *"Never Would Have Made It"*; however, I assure you that you will be stronger and wiser with the help of the Holy Spirit – your true guide on the journey.

> *If this were a course in restoration and transformation, this CD would be "required."*

Winans, CeCe, *"Thy Kingdom Come"*, 2008, www.cecewinans.com. This CD, especially Tracks 3-6 are timely sermons in song! I lived off of them during the 21 Days. They fed and nourished my spirit, soul, and body! The songs on the above tracks are so relevant to the "now" of God that when we read in *Charisma* that she was doing free concerts, we endeavored to get her to close out our 21 Day Journey: Not because she is a celebrity, but because the end of the 21 Day Journey is really a new beginning of a life filled with restoration and transformation! If this were a course in restoration and transformation, this CD would be *"required."*

Wilson, Andrea, *"In His Presence"*, 2005, Andrea Wilson Ministries, P.O. Box 906, Ellenwood, GA 30294, 404-376-0318, www.andreawilsonministries.org or at MySpace: www.myspace.com/andreawilson2. The first time I heard this young anointed woman of God, I knew she was more than a singer. With the first words from her mouth, looked at my wife and simply said – WOW! If you have an ear to hear, you can hea that her life and ministry has been tempered in the refining fire of His process. Hi process has created in her a passion for His presence and she wants everyone who wil to join her there – in His presence.

TEACHING SERIES

Brown, Earl, "*True Prayer Produces True Prosperity: God's Roadmap to Become A Kingdom Distributor of Wealth,*" (5 CDs), 2008, Giving People Hope, P.O. Box 92893 Lakeland, FL 33804-2893, www.hopecoaching.org. This is a five part series upor Job 22:21-30. There is a craze or phase in the church at present with a fascination to "*declare a thing and it shall be established unto you*" (Job 22:28). However, this series will dissect the entire context of that verse and show you how PAPA God is calling for a people who will learn the lessons of prophetic prayer and dare to become Kingdom Distributors of wealth. As we were concluding this series the Holy Spirit directed me to call people out in our church and to wash their feet during a Sunday morning service while they held a copy of "*The One Minute Millionaire*" in their lap. This series will help you to declare the "*instructions you receive from His mouth*". This manual would have never come into existence had I not "*received instructions from His mouth*" to declare a 21 Day Daniel Fast for rain. And, had I not heard the voice of the Holy Spirit through Mrs. Joyce Mitchell. I strongly recommend this series for business people, entrepreneurs and those who want to be.

> *...Pastor Letitia is clothed with an anointing that will release an impartation that quickens manifestation in your life.*

Stones, Letitia, "*The Call of the Kingdom: Intimacy, Internal Strength, Impact*" (4 CDs), 2008, Giving People Hope, P.O. Box 92893, Lakeland, FL 33804-2893, www.hopecoaching. org. As Pastor Letitia states in this series "*The Kingdom is an internal-eternal principle.*" In this four part series the Holy Spirit masterfully uses her as an instrument to demystify what it means to "*seek first the Kingdom of God....*" If you truly hunger and thirst to experience God's provisions in your life, your marriage, your family, your church, or your community – this series is for you! More importantly, if you want to understand the price to be prayed to experience the "*Intimate Friendship with God!*" that Bishop Francis talked about in the Foreword, this series will accelerate your passion to experience intimacy, inner strength and impact. *Most importantly,* **Pastor Letitia is clothed with an anointing that will release an impartation that quickens manifestation in your life**. When Pastor Letitia first ministered in our church, one of our young people said with great enthusiasm, "Pastor, she's better than you." Not only is she better – *she carries a unique anointing that is a precious and special gift to the Body of Christ!* Receive this teaching and experience restoration and transformation that will unlock and unleash the rivers of living water clogged in the womb of your spirit.

BOOKS

Brown, Earl R., *Help Me God! I Still Yearn For My Earthly Father's Affection,* Xulon Press: Longwood, FL, 2004.

> ***Don't let the title fool you***! This book will not only bring healing, restoration and transformation. It will serve as a catalyst to increase your intimacy with PAPA God. Also, what occurs in one part of your "***being***" affects the other parts. My discussion of the "***binding power***" of spirit, soul, and body will provide insight into the unique power of the Daniel Fast. The Chapter "*Kingdom Music Therapy*" alone is worth the investment.

Enlow, Johnny, *The Seven Mountain Prophecy,* Creation House: Lake Mary, FL, www.creationhouse.com, 2008.

> In 2006, before we started our church the Holy Spirit gave me Revelation Chapter 5 as our "Call to Worship" for our community. He had me studying the seven things that the "Worthy One" received and searching for insight into the "seven enemies" that the "sons of Israel" had to overcome to possess and occupy their promised land. While teaching our new member's course, "*Fulfilling Our Kingdom Responsibility,*" Pastor Letitia asked me if I had heard of or read this book. I said no. She said, I must get it for you and you must read it! As the Queen said of Solomon – this book answered all my questions concerning the "why" of the seven enemies and God's call to Revelation chapter 5. I believe this book answers all the foundational questions about ***God's call to train people to "ascend to the height of their assigned mountain*."**

I believe this book answers all the foundational questions about God's call to train people to "ascend to the height of their assigned mountain."

Francis, John, *Talitha Cumi: The Secrets of the Prayer Shawl,* Creation House: Lake Mary, FL, 2007.

> Whether you own a prayer shawl, want to own a prayer shawl or could care less about a prayer shawl – this book will open your understanding to the Word of God and His commandments and their role in prayer. His exploration of Jesus raising Jairus' daughter from the dead is alone worth the purchase price.

Johnson, Bill, Dreaming With God: Secrets to Redesigning Your World Through God's Creative Flow, Destiny Image: Shippensburg, PA, 2006.

> The end result of fasting and prayer is to partner with God in fulfilling what He has already promised. Even more importantly, fasting and prayer will help us to tap into the deep – seated desires of our heart and give us the confidence and courage to pursue them with passion. This book provides a roadmap to empower you and guide you to Designed Destiny by freeing you to truly partner with God as you "seek His face": "**have a conversation with Him.**"

McKnight, Jonathan L., *Prayer is a Must: A Spiritual Handbook to Prevail in*

Prayer, JLM Publishing: Orlando, FL 33835, 2008, www.jlmcknightministries.org, www.sanctuaryofpraise.org.

This small Big Book will explode your prayer life like a supersonic spiritual missile! It is a prayer restoration and transformation manual. The 120 Powerful prayer facts and declarations would be worth the purchase. However, it has seven life changing prayers in the book as well as a companion Prayer CD included. The CD alone would be worth the purchase price. The last seven days I listened to the prayers on CD every day, while exercising. **The power prayer thoughts in this manual are taken from this book**.

Prince, Derek, *Shaping History Through Prayer & Fasting: How Christians Can Change World Events Through the Simple, Yet Powerful Tools of Prayer and Fasting,* Derek Prince Ministries, P.O. Box 19501, Charlotte, NC 28219, 1973, www.derekprince.org.

If you're serious about biblical fasting and prayer and you can only afford to buy one book – this one is a must.

If you're serious about biblical fasting and prayer and you can only afford to buy one book – **this one is a must**. I'm on my second one and it is being held together by tape. PAPA God expects us to fast on purpose, with purpose, and for His purposes. **You will never need another book on fasting and prayer, other than your Bible**. Every person who is passionate about being a believing Believer should pray about this book being a constant companion. **All those who desire to ascend the heights of their assigned mountain should devour this book**.

Umidi, Joseph, *Transformational Coaching: Bridge Building that Impacts, Connects, and Advances the Ministry and the Marketplace,* Xulon Press: Longwood, FL, 2005.

I believe **Transformational Coaching is a technology for community transformation because it honors the unique design, desires, dreams and destiny of every person and is fueled by the life changing power of encouragement**. The cutting edge leader in the field of transformational coaching is LifeForming Leadership Coaching. This premier Christian coach training school is now in more than 20 countries with a curriculum that is in more than ten languages. This book provides the background, core values and philosophy of transformational coaching, from a Christian perspective. If you want to learn to leverage your conversations and listen people to their true greatness don't just purchase the book, contact LifeForming at www.lifeformingcoach.com or our licensed site at www.hopecoaching.org and experience coaching or become a coach.

ABOUT THE AUTHOR

Earl entered the Navy one year after graduating from high school. He worked his way from the "deck force" through many different sectors of the Navy but always in fields where he helped others. During his 20-year career he served as a Medical Specialist, Human Resource Management Specialist, Career Counselor, Navy Recruiter, Recruiting Manager, and Senior Enlisted Advisor. While in the Navy Earl was ordained as assistant pastor of the New Friendship Missionary Baptist Church in Jacksonville, Florida under the leadership of Rev. Dr. Aaron Neal in May 1983. In May of 1985 he became the pastor of Greater Faith Missionary Baptist church, a one-year-old congregation that was meeting in a small house in Mulberry, Florida. Earl's visionary leadership, motivational skills, and passion for people were personified when he left the Mulberry congregation in 1989 meeting in a 200-seat sanctuary, a two-story educational facility, ample parking, and a parsonage for the Pastor.

Currently, Earl is the Senior Pastor of Freely Forgiven Community Church in Lakeland, Florida: a center of life, hope, and purpose where people experience family, freedom, identity, and destiny. He has been married to Linda for 37 years. They have four children and six grandchildren. Some of his many accomplishments include:

- President, Nehemiah Church & Ministry Network and Giving People Hope Intl. Ministries
- Lifetime Member of the Graduate Schools of Coaching
- Lifetime Member of Coachville
- Certified LifeForming Leadership Coach & Coach Trainer
- Author & Motivational Speaker
- Resource Member, Association of Marriage & Family Ministry
- Faculty Administrator (Director of Adult and Continuing Education) at Norfolk State University for 3 years
- Served in numerous appointed and elected positions in church and civic organizations in America and Africa
- Holds degrees: BS & MA from Norfolk State University; BTH (Bachelor of Theology); MTH (Masters of Theology); PhD from International Seminary and a Doctor of Ministry in Leadership and Marriage and Family Ministry from Regent University
- Certified Human Behavior Consultant
- A Trained PREVENT (Personal Responsibility: Values, Education and Training) facilitator
- Trained in Fighting for Your Marriage: The PREP™ APPROACH and certified in PREPARE/ENRICH, both pre-marital and marriage enrichment programs
- A Seminar Director for PREPARE/ENRICH – training others in the use of the program
- A certified Family Wellness (Survival Skills for Healthy Families) instructor and has completed training to become a certified Family Mediator by the State Supreme Court of Virginia
- Licensed Instructor for PAIRS: practical skills for emotional literacy & extraordinary relationships

Made in the USA
Charleston, SC
14 December 2010